Derek Hyde
Knows Spooky
When He Sees It

To Kirill !

E Michael Lunsford

E. Michael Lunsford

Derek Hyde Knows Spooky

When He Sees It

E. Michael Lunsford

INTENSE PUBLICATIONS
www.INtensePublications.com

INtense Publications
Paperback ISBN: 978-1-947796-22-5
Derek Hyde Knows Spooky When He Sees It
Copyright © 2019 E. Michael Lunsford

This edition published by arrangement with INtense Publications LLC. The opinions expressed by the author are not necessarily those of INtense Publications LLC.

www.INtensePublications.com

Printed in U.S.A.

To Merlyn, the love of my life

Table of Contents

Home Creepy Home

DEREK FIGURED THERE MIGHT BE FAR WORSE THINGS IN life than being dragged off to live in a funeral home. For example, he could... um...

Okay, here's one. He could have his brains eaten alive and slurped down by cranky, overworked zombies who haven't had their morning coffee.

Or how about this? He could be stuffed into a spin dryer at Leo's Laundromat & Hideous Stain Removal Service and set to Extra Dry/Huge Load.

But Derek wasn't eaten, and he definitely wasn't spin dried, either. Just driven to the sleepy town of Littleburp in the family car (actually, an old yellow school bus), and then to a really unfortunate and grossly undesirable address: 1313 Slimeytoes Lane.

Still, it felt like the worst day of his life (so far) as the bus splashed its way through a crazy thunderstorm. His mom and dad kept trying to keep his spirits up by singing their favorite, most embarrassing song: *Poopy Head, Poopy Head, Don't You Be a Poopy Head.*

It didn't help.

It was bad enough his adoptive parents had pulled Derek out of his seventh-grade class and away from all his friends to limp across the country in a broken-down school bus on this Journey to Nowhere. Much worse was the idea of moving him into a spooky old mansion they planned to convert into a funeral home.

You see, both his parents were funeral directors. Morticians. Undertakers.

On this blustery autumn day, noisy brakes slowed them to a squealing stop in front of their new home. Derek watched through his rain-streaked window as a flash of lightning lit the sky behind the most frightening mansion he'd ever seen.

It had towers. With bars on the windows.

It also had spikes on the roof. And a creaky old weathervane made in the shape of a French guillotine. (Either that, or it might have been a cheese grater with a thumb hole. Derek couldn't tell for sure.)

Anyway, it was worse than eerie. This place was horrific. Goosebumps popped up all over his body. He swallowed twice to wet his scratchy throat.

As if that weren't freaky enough, someone had planted an ancient cemetery right next door, and beyond that a small, abandoned building with a peeling but elaborately painted sign that read: *Our Lady of Immaculate Kitchens*.

Derek read it twice.

A damp guy with a clipboard in one hand and an umbrella in the other rushed down from the mansion's front porch and scampered across the lawn to greet them. The glasses perched on his nose were fogged by the same rain that drenched his wrinkled pin-striped suit.

Standing outside the bus, he shouted, "Mr. and Mrs. ...um..." He swiped his coat sleeve at his glasses and squinted at the clipboard. "Hyde, isn't it? Welcome to your new abode."

Derek's skinny dad pulled a lever to open the bus door and bounded down the short rubber steps to pump the poor man's umbrella hand. "Glad to meet you, Mr... uh..."

"Duckworthy," the man said. "Horace Duckworthy, at your service. From the Unreal Real Estate Agency."

"Mr. Duckworthy. My pleasure. I'm Jack L. Hyde, and this is my wife, Formalda." He gestured toward the bus.

Formalda waved from her seat. "Howdy!"

"And this is our son, Derek." Out of the side of his mouth he added, "Actually, our adopted son."

Derek waved from the seat behind his mom. "Hi, Mr. Duckworthy."

"Hello, young man." The realtor turned to Derek's dad and murmured, "There's a slight problem I should tell you about…"

Before he could finish, four shrieking police cars and a battered old ambulance zigzagged around the corner, jumped the curb in front of the mansion and ended in a bumper-car jumble all over the yard. Police and paramedics jumped out and charged through the front door.

Mr. Duckworthy absentmindedly tilted his umbrella to shield Derek's dad from the rain. They both stared, open-mouthed.

Sounds of scuffles and shouted instructions erupted from inside the mansion. Words like, "He's over here!" and "No, this way. Grab him!"

A white-haired kid wearing dark jeans and a black T-shirt exploded through the front door. Despite his abnormally high forehead and dark eye bags, he looked to be about Derek's age, but taller. A faster runner, too.

Officers in blue and paramedics in bright green reflector vests galloped behind the kid. They would've caught him, but he made a home-base slide right under the bus.

Derek stood up to see where he'd gone as the cops dashed around both ends of the bus to cut him off. The kid must've anticipated that though, because he reappeared at Derek's window, slapping at the glass and yelling, "Let me in!"

Too late. A policeman jumped at him, grabbed his arm and clapped on a pair of handcuffs before the kid could slip from their grasp again.

As they hauled him away, their struggling young prisoner pointed two fingers at his own eyes, then pointed them at Derek.

Great. Nice welcome. I'm here five minutes and already made my first enemy.

The kid kept glaring at Derek as paramedics shoved him into the ambulance, then piled in after him. With sirens wailing, everybody drove off the front lawn and down the street.

The realtor let out a couple of *tsk-tsk* sounds. "Well, I guess you'll have a little lawn-patching to do…"

Derek's mom bounded out of the bus wearing her favorite flower print dress, a floppy hat and a giant grin. "That was thrilling," she shrieked. She punched his dad on the arm. "And you said this town was boring."

"Ow." Dad grabbed his arm and gave her a pained expression. "I didn't say boring, exactly. I think I said sleepy, or slow, something like that." He turned to Mr. Duckworthy. "What was that all about, anyway?"

The realtor returned a sheepish smile. "That's the problem I almost mentioned. That little monster escaped from the city's benevolent Department for Uncontrollably Delinquent Snot-noses. DUDS for short. The police always search for him here first."

"But who is he?" Dad asked.

"I think his name is Norval or Orville, something like that. He's the son of Mr. and Mrs. Nussbaum, the wealthy couple who used to own this mansion. This is the fifth time they've had to drag him out. I'm afraid he's not handling the sale of his home quite as well as his parents."

Dad scratched his head. "So where are his parents?"

"His parents? Oh, they're dead."

"They're—"

"Dead. Yep. Seems one day they bought their little boy a chemistry set and—well, you know how kids are." The realtor glanced at Derek. "Apparently, he threw in some chemicals that didn't come with the set and accidentally blew up his parents with one giant KA-BOOM! Too bad. It was just as they were getting ready for a grocery run to the Piggly Wiggly."

The realtor turned a little red, then continued, "Oh, but don't worry. We cleaned up the mess. It was pretty devastating; I have to say. Charred walls, burnt ceiling and a big hole in the floor. Not to mention," he leaned forward to whisper, "well, you know, the guts and stuff."

He beamed. "But we rose to the challenge, all right, I can tell you that. Got that place all spruced up and ready for the open house in record time."

Leaning closer, he added, "And don't worry about all those rumors regarding any old gruesome, grisly, ghosts haunting the place. I'm sure that's idle gossip. Watercooler chit-chat. Vicious slander. Nothing to worry about at all."

"Oh, that's all right then," Dad said. He offered his arm to Mom. "Shall we *entré*, my dear?"

"*Avec mucho plaisir.*" Mom grabbed the hem of her dress with one hand and placed the other on Dad's wrist. Together they strode to the front door with all the sweet pride of new home ownership.

Dad shouted over his shoulder, "Coming Derek?"

Derek sighed, climbed down from the bus and followed as Dad scooped Mom up in his arms and carried her over the threshold to a loud series of giggles.

Inside, Mom overflowed with oohs and aahs as she waltzed through the living room, her hands clapping like a seal at the circus. "This is stupid-pendous," she gurgled, "mega-magical. Check out that parquet floor. And the gi-normous chandelier." She spun around. "Oh Jack, you sweet thing. It's in-flipping-credible. You've surpassed my lowest expectations."

Dad beamed like a baby getting ice cream. "I'm so glad you like it, Pumpkin. I have to admit, I was a little worried, snatching it up sight unseen, with nothing but a floor plan."

"Well, so was *I*. But *look* at it. It's everything we've ever wanted."

Derek wasn't so sure. For one thing, it stank of burnt wood, but not in a nice outdoor campfire kind of way. It was more like an indoor, three-alarm, melt-your-face, roast-the-cat, devil's inferno sort of smell.

A shiver wiggled up his spine. "Are you sure there're no ghosts?"

His dad tut-tutted. "You're not afraid, are you?"

Derek shuddered. "What, me? No way, 'course not."

Dad draped his arm around Derek's shoulder. "True courage isn't being fearless, son." He took on a more solemn tone and whispered, "It's being afraid, but not making poopy in your pants."

"Oh. Okay. Thanks, Dad."

Cobwebs sprouted everywhere, like moldy cotton candy. Derek couldn't help noticing how the deep reddish walls sucked the afternoon light from every room. As if that weren't enough, a vicious wind wailed down the chimney and the doors creaked louder than the floorboards. Even the cabinets in the old-fashioned kitchen squeaked painful complaints.

Of course, not to be outdone, gnarled branches from the trees outside licked, clicked and scraped at the windows.

"This will be awesome-possum for Halloween," Derek's mom gushed. "Absolutely the right amount of spooky."

"More like the wrong amount of creepy," Derek mumbled as he quivered his way to the foot of the grand staircase. He gazed up at a scary-looking second floor. "Is my room up there?"

Dad answered in a grave, fake-British-butler voice. "Of course, Master Hyde," He gave a mock bow. "Your Majesty will find *our* bedroom on the left, a den in the middle, and *your* room is the one on the right."

Derek didn't wait for more instructions. He put his hands in his pockets, headed up the stairs, turned right and stopped short at a handwritten sign on the door:

DO NOT ENTER

ON PAIN OF DEATH AND DISMEMBERMENT.

NOT IN THAT ORDER.

Great. He slowly turned the knob and peeked inside.

The floor, ceiling, bookcases, closet door and moth-eaten curtains were all black as fresh asphalt. So were the walls, except for some scrawled, dripping red messages:

BEWARE THE JABBERWOCK

FEAR THE NIGHT

AVOID THE THIRTEENTH

KEEP OFF THE GRASS

LATHER, RINSE, REPEAT

Dude. What the what? He took a nervous breath and stepped into the room, already wondering how many cans of paint it would take to change everything to another color. Any color. Breathless blue. Ominous orange. Pig-belly pink.

Derek peeked into the closet. The single black rod had only one ebony-wood hanger. He reached up to remove it, but it wouldn't budge. *Weird.* As he wrestled with it, the back wall of the closet slid away to reveal a set of wooden steps. A long string dangled from a single light bulb hanging over the stairs.

He couldn't stop his hand from shaking, but he pulled the string anyway. The bulb lit a circular stairway curving up and to the right. He couldn't tell where it ended.

The colder air in the shaft made him gasp. He wrinkled his nose at the musty smell.

He gulped and stood up straighter. Fists clenched, he started up the stairs, announcing out loud, "I'm *not* afraid, I'm *not* afraid."

A moment later, he hurried back down again, whispering in a faster, much smaller voice, "I *am* afraid, I *am* afraid, I *am* afraid..."

He'd already stepped safely out of the closet before he stopped to mentally slap himself. What was he doing? Trophies for Bravest Kid in the Face of Dire Disaster and Certain Catastrophe weren't awarded for running away. *Awesome. No choice. I have to face this. Or maybe if I back into it...*

With a deep sigh he turned, stepped into the closet and white-knuckled the handrail as he crept his way back up the rickety stairs.

2

Who Needs Sleeping Bags?

SWAYING LIGHT FROM THE HANGING BULB ROCKED HIS shadow on the walls all the way to the top. Finally, he bumped against the underside of an odd trapdoor that seemed weirdly out of place.

His knees shook and his hands felt clammy. *Okay. That's as far as I go. This is where I go get Mom and Dad.*

But wait. He couldn't give in to his fears. Not now. He couldn't simply head back down the stairs with a reluctant *oh well*… He needed to get hold of himself, get a backbone, reach up and push the trapdoor open. Nothing to get freaked about. It was a trapdoor. A simple trapdoor. A creepy, cobweb-decorated Portal to Unbearable Terror, that's all. No problem.

If only that realtor guy hadn't talked about ghosts haunting the mansion…

He shook his head. His hands shook, too. But hey, paranoia wouldn't get the better of him. Derek stretched one unsteady hand to the trapdoor and gave it a tentative push. It wouldn't move.

He shoved with both hands. No luck. Stepping higher, he wedged his shoulder and head against it. At last, the trapdoor gave way, gradually lifted and crashed on its other side in a billow of ancient dust.

Derek stuck his head through the opening and glanced around like a terrified turtle.

No ghosts.

No moaning or rattling chains, either. Only thunder and the sound of rain performing a random tap dance on the roof.

This was some attic, though. Not just musty and old, but filled with weird and long-forgotten belongings. Magazines lay in crooked piles directly in front of him. At first, Derek thought they might be comic books, but as his eyes adjusted to the light from a single attic window, he realized they were all about military gear and weapons.

A rocking horse cast a menacing shadow in one corner—except it wasn't a horse. More like a large, hairy dog on rockers. Or a wolf. A wolf with dead, glassy eyes.

In another corner sprawled a collection of gray metal boxes labeled with scribbled titles, like PERFECT REVENGE and GETTING ODD —GETTING EVEN.

Next to that sat a large cardboard box with a paper sign taped to its side that read: HALLOWEEN JUNK.

He decided to try the Halloween box first. A jumbled string of black and orange lights covered a set of miniature coffins, small plastic pumpkins and huge hairy spiders. His fingers traced the rubbery pile of masks of zombies, gorillas, vampires and a few U.S. presidents.

Derek crept to the metal boxes and pulled out a disconcerting collection of toys: a broken slingshot, two bicycle chains, plastic hand grenades, rubber knives, three water pistols and a pink-handled jump rope tied in a noose.

So that white-haired kid who used to occupy his new room was obviously nice and wholesome, a model student, clearly best friend material. *Yeah, right.*

At least Derek's hands weren't shaking anymore. Nothing to fear here, only the creepy leftovers of a weird kid. Who did lose both his parents, after all.

As he began to relax, a white mist seeped up from the floorboards, joined by the strong stench of rotten eggs. He backed away so quickly, he bumped up against the rocking-wolf. Then he wheeled around, surprised by the feeling of coarse fur.

Unfortunately, he must have startled the wolf, too. Its head slowly rotated in his direction.

Derek turned a bloodless white as the enormous jaws opened and the wolf's saliva-dripping mouth gave off a low, rumbling growl.

Derek's knees buckled. He scrambled backward on all fours like a panicked crab. Then he rolled into a ball, head ducked and covered, and let out an involuntary whimper. He froze, already expecting the wolf's jaws clamped around his neck.

After long, shaky seconds of painful silence, he peeked under one arm. The wolf's head now faced forward, its mouth closed, its eyes glassy again.

That was all it took. Derek dove through the open trapdoor and fumble-stumbled his way to the bottom of the steps, out of the bedroom closet and down the main staircase into the wide hall.

Charging from room to room, gasping for air, he tried to keep his heart from exploding out of his chest. This was another world. A horrible, horrendous, *hairy* world. Not exactly fun.

He finally found his parents in the kitchen. They stood between the island sink and an antique gas stove, staring down at a large simmering pot.

Mom beamed at her frazzled boy. "There you are, my young prince. Perfectly in time for some late dinner. We're having pickle-and-popcorn soup. Pull up a stool."

He tried to catch his breath. "M-m-mom, D-d-dad. I found… a secret panel… a stairway to the attic… a wolf…"

Dad laughed. "A wolf in the attic? Did he threaten to huff and puff and blow the house down?"

"I'm not kidding… It was a wolf. On rockers. But it snarled at me. And growled."

"So *not* off his rocker, then," Dad said.

"Right. Wait, what?"

"I wouldn't worry, Son." Dad handed three empty bowls to Mom. "It's probably your imagination. You're tired, from the long trip."

Mom dipped a ladle into the pot. "Or maybe not. This could be wonderful. A paranormal experience on our very first night." She put a steaming bowl on the counter in front of Derek. *"Bon appetit."*

Derek pushed the bowl away. "You don't get it. I could have been attacked. Chomped into pieces. Eaten alive."

"That's nice, dear." Mom finished ladling the soup into the other two bowls. She and Dad both pulled stools up to the island counter and sat down.

Derek pulled on his dad's arm. "Don't you want to *see?* You should go up there. Without me, but—"

Dad put down his spoon. "All right son, don't get your knickers in a twist. I'll go." He turned to Mom. "You'd better stay here where it's safe, Dreamboat."

"No way. If we have apparitions, I want to see." She glanced down at what she was wearing. "How's my dress? Am I presentable?"

"You look amazing, Platypus."

She pushed away from the counter. "Last one there is a barf bag!"

She beat them to the main staircase, up to the second floor and into Derek's new bedroom. They caught up with her standing in the middle of the room, staring all around. "So where's your mysterious ladder to the attic?"

"It's in the closet, but it's not a ladder." Derek opened the closet door, pulled on the ebony coat hanger and stood aside.

Their eyes went wide as the back panel opened.

"Whoa," Dad said.

"Double whoa," Mom echoed.

Dad craned his head to see better, but Mom pushed past him and headed up the stairs first. Squeaky boards creaked with her every step. Dad followed her and was halfway out of sight before he leaned back down to ask Derek, "Aren't you coming?"

Derek futzed with his belt. "Oh no, that's okay. I've already seen it."

"Suit yourself."

Derek held his breath as he listened to their clomping in the attic above, followed by murmured voices and a short squeal. He froze. Part of him wanted to rush to their aid. But a wiser part of him suggested being frozen might not be all that bad.

It seemed like forever before they finally returned.

"Well, we saw the rocking-wolf," Dad said. "But it's not moving at all. I even kicked it, and it didn't budge."

"Yes, but I saw something even better," Mom offered. "A box of cool decorations for Halloween. How lucky is that?"

"The wolf didn't snarl or growl or anything?" Derek wasn't sure if it felt right to be disappointed.

"Nope," Dad answered. "Great attic, though. Love the secret staircase."

Derek couldn't believe it. Did they think he just made this all up? That he didn't actually see what he said he saw?

A few minutes later, as they sat at their evening meal, he fiddled with his soup spoon. "So you didn't smell anything bad, or see something like a fog?"

Mom wrinkled her nose. "Uhn-uhn, not a mist. I guess that's what you get when you go ghost hunting on an empty stomach. Dig in."

They slurped their food as Derek insisted, "But honest, I did see..."

Dad pointed his fork at Derek. "Now come on, young man, you need your strength. Besides, it's getting late. We need to figure out our sleeping arrangements."

Derek stopped procrastinating and ate a few bites on automatic pilot, not really listening. Then Dad's words sank in. He mumbled past the food in his mouth, "Wait, aren't we sleeping in the bus? There're no beds in the house."

Mom's head shot up. "You know, he's right. Silly me. We should've brought sleeping bags, but all we have is blankets. That won't be very comfortable on a cold hardwood floor."

Dad gave a smug grin. "I thought of that, and I have a solution."

"What?"

"Body bags."

"Body bags?"

"Body bags. They're in the back of the bus, in a box labeled CADAVER GEAR."

Mom caught on. "My brilliant husband, how clever you are. Of course. They're almost like sleeping bags."

Derek's mouth flapped open and shut. "You're kidding, right?"

"No, your father's idea is great. You wrap yourself in a blanket, then zip yourself up in a body bag. It'll be perfect."

Derek mumbled to himself, "Perfect."

Dad reached over to ruffle Derek's hair. "That's our boy."

After dinner, Dad brought in blankets, pillows and body bags from the bus. He dropped some off in the master bedroom. Then he and Mom escorted Derek to his room where they wrapped and zipped him up.

Derek felt a little like a fly being web-wrapped by a pair of loving spiders.

He wiggled on the floor, his shivering arms pinned inside the stiff vinyl bag. "It's cold. Doesn't this place have a furnace?"

Dad shook his head. "It does, but I couldn't figure out the pilot light. I'll call somebody about it tomorrow."

Mom clucked her tongue. "You poor dear, what you need is a hat."

Derek shrugged. "I don't have a hat."

"Here, I brought some of your clothes from the bus." She slung a bag from her shoulder, reached in and plucked out some jockey shorts. "How about a pair of your underpants?"

"I'm *not* wearing underpants on my head."

Mom sulked a little as she put them away. "It's not like they haven't been washed..."

They left Derek alone in his room. As they turned off the light and closed his door, Mom whispered, "Goodnight." Over her shoulder, Dad added, "Don't let the vampires bite."

That was all Derek needed. No sleep for him. For an hour he tossed and turned. He kept thinking about his experience in the attic. But his parents didn't see a thing. Maybe Mom was right, he shouldn't have gone exploring on an empty stomach.

He lay there listening to the creaks and groans of the old mansion and the *slap, slap-slap* of a shutter somewhere at the opposite end of the house. Then his ears perked up. That was a thumping noise. He sat up and cocked his head to listen more intently. There it was again. What was it?

He felt clammy again, but not just his hands this time. His whole body.

He worked one hand out of his body bag and grabbed the zipper. He unzipped down to his waist, squirmed the rest of the way out and stood up, still listening for that sound. It came from above.

Oh, no. Not the attic again. He couldn't mount those stairs one more time. But if he didn't, he'd never convince his parents that this place was really haunted. He shuddered.

If only he had a weapon to take with him. Like the closet pole, that would work. He opened the closet and wrestled with the pole to pull it out, but that only activated the sliding door. He slowly stuck his head in and squinted up the spiral staircase.

The thumping sound started up again. He held his breath, pulled the string to the hanging light and crept up the steps. Doing his best to imitate a cautious cat. Or a timid tarantula.

As he poked his head through the trap door at the top, the sound halted. He rotated around a full 360 degrees but couldn't see anything unusual. If you didn't count the rocking-wolf.

He stepped up into the attic, half-expecting a hot breath on his collar or a bony hand on his shoulder. Nothing.

Derek noticed for the first time a dormer window at the far end of the attic, filtering in a hint of moonlight. He edged past the boxes and magazines. Then he pulled his shirt sleeve over one hand to wipe enough dirt away from the window to make a porthole to peek through.

Everything looked normal. A dusty magnolia tree at the edge of the lawn below swayed in the night breeze, waving at the yellow school bus parked in the street.

He gagged as a sudden stench of rotten eggs filled the air. A freaky mist seeped up from the floorboards, swirled in place for a minute, then transformed into a couple of ghosts. One wore a rumpled suit and the other sported an elegant but soiled black dress topped off with a pearl necklace. There was only one thing missing. They had no heads.

Derek's heart went into drum solo mode. The part where the drummer goes manic.

The swaying apparitions moved in a kind of clumsy stumble as they groped and flailed their way straight toward Derek.

He flattened himself against the window, arms up in surrender, but they kept coming.

Derek slid to one side, then backed into a small space between the slanted ceiling and the rough floorboards. His breath came in short gasps, and he sweated like a dripping showerhead.

The headless ghosts shuffled and slouched their way toward the window, arms outstretched as if feeling for invisible walls. They reached the window and disappeared. Derek couldn't tell if they went through it or simply vanished at the boundary. Anyway, they were gone.

He charged for the trap door and practically dove through it. He lost his balance twice as he lurched down the steps, out of his closet and down the hall to his parents' room.

He found them lying in their body bags under an enormous stained glass window decorated with a portrait of Saint George lancing a dragon. Weird.

"M-m-mom, D-d-dad. I heard a sound… They're in the attic… Two ghosts…"

Dad laughed. "Two ghosts, huh? You really saw them?"

"Yes, and they were headless. No heads. Beheaded."

Mom sat up. "Did they come at you, dear?"

"Yes. Right at me. Face to face. Well actually, face to *no*-face."

Dad unzipped his body bag and struggled out. "You honestly saw a ghost?"

"*Two* ghosts. No skulls. See-through."

"Right." Dad went to the window seat. "No problem. I came prepared." He lifted the seat, grabbed something and headed for the light switch. When the light came on, he stood in front of Derek holding an old sledgehammer.

"Wait, we have a sledgehammer?" Derek asked.

"We do now. I found it in the basement. Or cellar. Or maybe it's more of a dungeon."

"Wait, we have a dungeon?"

"Don't worry, Son. I got this. This is a job for the man of the house."

Mom stood up, still in her body bag. "Hold on a second there, Buckaroo. The woman of the house isn't going to stay here, shivering like a sea slug. I'm going too." She unzipped herself and stepped out wearing polka-dot pajamas. She stepped behind Dad. "You have the sledgehammer, so you go first."

Derek stayed put as his parents tiptoed, single file, down the hall and into his room.

He waited for an eternity, gradually regaining his regular breathing. His clothes felt sticky, drenched in sweat.

They finally reappeared. Dad returned the old sledgehammer to the window seat, shaking his head. "Sorry, Son. No ghosts. Everything looks the same as before."

"Sweetie, maybe you should sleep with us, here in the master bedroom," Mom offered. "We never heard any sounds from here."

Derek nodded. "I guess you're right." He looked back toward the door and let out a small, shaky sigh.

Half an hour later, the lights out again, Derek rolled over on one side, but that didn't feel right. He tried the other side. No good. He lay on his back.

All this moving around made his plastic body bag rustle.

Dad's drowsy voice broke through the darkness. "Can't you sleep, Son?"

"No. I keep thinking about the wolf, giving off that low growl. And those fangs and glassy eyes. And the ghosts. Creepy, spooky ghosts, haunting the attic. Without any heads. And stumbling around, like they're looking for something. Know what I mean?"

There was no answer. Only the sound of two peaceful parents, quietly snoring in the dark.

Visitors from the Attic

THE NEXT MORNING, DEREK WOKE WITH A PLEASANT THOUGHT . *Things always feel better after a good night's sleep.* If only he could get one.

But hey, what could be so bad? He lived in a funeral home with completely kooky parents, his bedroom was a testament to the latest trends in Goth, and their attic was haunted by a couple of ghosts. And a stuffed wolf that doesn't know it's dead. What's not to like?

Derek trudged down the stairs hoping for a reasonable breakfast. From the kitchen, he could hear his mom humming *The Yellow Rose of Texas*, a song she learned at last year's mortician's conference in Dallas. Dad whistled along as he whisked a bowl of pancake batter. "Good morning, Son. Sleep well?"

"Morning, Dad. Not so much."

"Well, I slept like a top," Dad volunteered. "Not the spinning kind, of course."

"Me too," Mom added. "Except, my body bag was a little smelly." She turned to Dad. "Was that a new one, or used?"

"Used, I think..." Dad said. "But not for long. How about some breakfast, Son?"

"Sure, what're we having?"

Mom waved a spatula. "It's my latest invention. I call it the Welcome to Our New Funeral Home breakfast. We're having maggot milk, tombstone-shaped pancakes with R.I.P. written in chocolate syrup, and mixed fruit in miniature coffins."

Derek gagged a little but managed to hide it. "Yummy…"

As they all dug in, Dad ran his finger down his to-do list. "Okay, as soon as we clean up here, I'm off to Otto's Ominous Signs Shop to get the sign for our funeral home. You guys need to stay here for delivery of some of the heavier equipment. Oh, and the display coffin. That's coming today, too."

Mom talked through her last mouthful of pancake. "Goody, I can't wait." She stood up with a twirl, grabbed several dishes and started scrubbing them in the sink.

After returning to his bedroom, Derek opened the closet door to see if any dead spirits happened to be floating down the attic stairs. He needn't have bothered though since the secret panel was closed. Probably the default setting.

He wandered to his bedroom window to check out the view. Then wished he hadn't. The old cemetery next door seemed a lot closer in the daylight. Great. Could his life *get* any more terrifying?

Derek sat cross-legged in the middle of the floor, chin on fist. He needed to think. This was not going to work. Even if he didn't get night sweats from his fear of coffins and bodies, actually sleeping in a funeral home had to be unhealthy. No, scratch that. Sleeping in a *haunted* funeral home was unhealthy.

It was official. He had the all-time, championship, head-of-the-class, blue ribbon, most insanely horrendous living situation of any kid in modern times.

All I want is a nice place to live. Is that too much to ask? I have to do something about this. But what?

The sound of a truck pulling up outside brought him out of his Murky Tar Pit of Doom and Despair. He moped down the main staircase to open the front door after the doorbell played a perky Mexican tune: *La Cucaracha.*

Two towering giants in gray overalls stood on the front stoop. The stouter giant peered at his clipboard. "Delivery for 1313… uh… Slimeytoads or Stinkytoes or something-something Lane."

"Okay, you can bring it in here." Derek swung the door wider. A large, highly polished coffin with ornate handles graced the front porch.

The men snatched up both ends of the coffin as if it were an empty canoe and maneuvered their way into the main hall. "Where d'ya want it?"

Mom came bustling out of the kitchen, wiping her hands on her apron. "How about over here by the window?"

"It doesn't have a body in it, does it?" Derek didn't really want an answer.

The two men responded with puzzled looks. They placed the coffin where Mom pointed. The skinnier giant grabbed the clipboard, glanced at Derek and ran his finger down the voucher. His shoulders relaxed. "No body. Only one Premium Deluxe Display Casket with Brass Accoutrements. Sorry."

Derek shrugged. "Maybe next time."

The giant gave him a blank stare. "Sign here."

Mom moved in, signed the receipt and took her copy of the voucher. "Thank you so much. It's exactly what we needed. Thank you. Thank you."

As they left, she nibbled at her finger. "You know, until our furniture arrives, the coffin might make for a more comfortable bed than my body bag. If we only had two more…"

"Wait," Derek countered. "You want to *sleep* in there?"

"Oh, you're right, what am I thinking? I might drool all over that beautiful silk lining and ruin it." She headed back to the kitchen muttering, "No, it's much better if we use it to eat on, till our dining table gets delivered."

He started to argue, but… Well, he couldn't say he was exactly surprised by her logic.

He strolled outside to stare at the front of the house. In spite of the fresh air from last night's rain, the property looked as creepy as before. The crooked trees on either side seemed to be standing guard and the peeling white paint gave the mansion that wonderful lived-in-by-ghouls look.

Gazing up, he almost wet his pants. The headless torsos of two ghostly figures stood in the attic window. Derek's pointing finger shook and his mouth opened and shut like a suffocating fish.

At that moment, the old school bus drove up. Derek sprinted across the lawn, pried open the doors of the bus and sputtered, "Dad, Dad. You have to see. Two ghosts, headless—"

He pointed to the top of the mansion, but only an old frayed curtain billowed in the open attic window. No ghosts.

Dad slipped down the short steps of the bus and shaded his eyes to stare up at the house. "I don't see anything."

Derek slumped. "They're gone. But they *were* there, I promise."

"Oh well, maybe we'll see them later." Dad moved around the bus and opened the rear door. "In the meantime, why don't you give me a hand with these signs?"

Derek sighed, then helped his dad unload two beautifully carved and painted wooden signs from the bus. Together they struggled with them to the porch. The first sign read

HYDE FUNERAL HOME

…and the second sign read

& USED COFFIN OUTLET

Derek scratched his head. "You're planning to sell *used* coffins?"

Dad chewed on his lip. "Well, you never know… Maybe…"

It took both of them to erect the signs, one above the other. Derek cringed to see that they actually made the place look like a real funeral home. *Bummer.* He squared his shoulders. Right. Time to discuss the mansion's apparitions. "Um… Dad…"

Dad stopped admiring their handiwork. "What's up?"

"Those two ghosts. I mean, they're really here. It's not a story. And I was wondering... Is it such a great idea to move into a haunted funeral home?"

"Oh, that. Not to worry, Son. If we do have ghosts, we'll get the place exterminated, or exorcised, or excremated. One of those 'ex' words. Don't give it another thought."

"But Dad..."

"Come on, I need your help in the embalming room." He started up the lawn.

Derek caught up and touched his dad's arm. "We have an embalming room?"

"It used to be a library, but we thought it'd be super for cold storage and body preparation. We might name it something more appealing, though. What do you think of this? The Restful Sleep Room."

"Sure. Perfect."

Once inside, Derek got an idea. "Dad, could I borrow your phone? For a minute?"

"Sure. Want to look something up?"

"No, I want to take some pictures of the house."

"Now, why didn't I think of that?" Dad wriggled the phone out of his front pants pocket and handed it over. "Great idea, Son. A record of our first morning in the new house."

"Right. Exactly. And then maybe *I* could have a phone? Someday soon?"

"A phone for you? Of course. Absolutely. As soon as our new funeral home takes off. You have my word on it."

Dad spat on his hand and thrust it toward Derek—who winced a little before shaking hands. As soon as his dad turned away, he wiped his palm on his pants leg.

He took a couple of pics of the main hall, then climbed up the central staircase, taking snapshots above and below as he went. He sauntered into his room and shut the door.

Now comes the hard part. Up to that freaky attic. Again. And me with no weapon. Unbearably scary, but he had no choice. Not if he hoped to get a picture of the ghosts. That would be real proof. And if he provided photographic evidence, what else could his parents do? They'd *have* to agree; this was no place for a growing boy. Time to move away. Far, far away.

He pried open the closet door and pulled on the coat hanger.

The black panel slid aside as soundlessly as before, as if to graciously invite him to please proceed into the Welcoming Jaws of Horror and Ignominious Death. *Nice.*

He stood tall and tried to swallow. If only he could calm his trembling knees.

Derek put his foot on the first of the wobbly steps and tried to focus. Assuming he wasn't captured and summarily dismembered, he might get a snapshot of the ghosts. Before running for his life, that is.

As it turned out, he didn't have to go up. Before he could take a second step, a rancid smell wafted down from the attic, followed by an eerie mist. And the sound of a couple of clumsy, staggering ghosts, feeling their way down the stairs.

He scrambled backward, trying not to trip over his own feet. With quivering hands, he brought the phone up to his eyes. He stared at the display. No ghosts.

The phone showed the wooden stairs, but otherwise, its screen was empty. Derek glanced up. There they were. Headless corpses stepping off the last step and into the closet. They came at him, arms reaching out and hands waving in the air.

Desperate, he rushed from the closet, slammed the door and backed up.

That didn't stop them. The two ghosts walked through it as if it weren't there.

A stifled scream struggled to escape his throat, but no sound came. He couldn't breathe. He fell to his knees.

The ghosts stumbled closer and closer. Then they groped their way right through him with a wet SWOOSH, leaving him covered with a noxious, pale green ectoplasm.

He was soaked. Drenched. Slimed.

Derek wiped the shimmering green goop from his eyes in time to see the ghosts blundering to the far bedroom wall. Where they disappeared.

That did it. Derek charged out of the room, raced down the main staircase and blasted through the mansion's front door. He darted his head left and right, frantic to figure out where to run next. A strong hand grabbed his shoulder. He jerked his head up to see—his dad.

"What's wrong, Son? You seem a little upset." Dad looked him up and down. "And why are you covered in lime Jell-O?"

"I saw the ghosts again! They're not in the attic anymore. They came down the closet stairs. Then they went for me. They slimed me!"

"They did?" With the tip of his fingers, Dad scooped a bit of ectoplasm from Derek's cheek and put it to his tongue. "Hmm. Tastes sort of musky, like ground-up spiders. Or maybe earthworms. But kind of sickly sweet, too."

"Yuck! Don't *eat* it."

Dad chuckled. "I have to hand it to you, Son. This is your best joke yet." He wiped his hand on his shirt. "You really had me going, for a minute there."

"But it's *not* a joke. They came down from the attic. I'm not kidding. We have to get out of here."

Dad looked down at the phone in Derek's hand. "Ah, then you must have evidence. I assume you got a photo?"

"*No*. No photo. But only because they didn't show up on the screen. You have to believe me—"

"Of course I believe you. Sure I do. Tell you what. You give me my phone back, go get cleaned up and—I know." Dad raised his right hand. "I solemnly promise to keep my sledgehammer handy, just in case. And you let me know when you see those mean old ghosts again."

Derek knew when he was being humored. But what could he do?

Later that evening, his little family sat at their newly-delivered coffin to enjoy a sumptuous meal of artichoke hearts and mystery meat.

Except for Derek. He only moved his food around on his plate. Finally, he lowered his fork and tried to give his parents a look of indifference. "So I was thinking… I bet we could do a lot better than this old place, what with the dead wolf and sliming ghosts and all. Just sayin'."

Mom stopped salting her meat. "Why, Derek. I'm gob-smacked. Don't you like your new bedroom?"

"It's not that. It's the previous occupants. Only, they're not so previous. More like current. Seems a little crowded for one mansion, don't you think?"

Dad gave him a fatherly smile. "Say, we have plenty of room. Bunches and barrels."

Mom agreed. "Scads and oodles."

Dad added, "And wait'll you see your new school. You'll never guess what it's called."

"Ooo, ooo, I know that one," Mom enthused. "It's the Heddy S. Kidd Middle School."

Derek cupped a hand around one ear. "The—"

"The Heddy S. Kidd Middle School. It's only a couple of miles away, a quick bus ride."

"So there's a school bus?" Derek asked.

Mom speared another artichoke and transferred it to her plate. "Oh no, we're off the route. But *we* can take you, every day. In *our* bus."

Derek waved his hands frantically. "Oh no, please no. That'd be too much." He turned to his dad. "Why do we have to ride around in a big yellow school bus anyway? Couldn't we trade it in for a decent family car?"

Mom's face brightened and she sat up straight. "He's right. If you think about it, it's not the best kind of vehicle to keep parked in front of our new funeral home."

Dad stopped eating. "I see what you mean. It doesn't give the somber, respectful vibe we should present as morticians. What do you say, Sweetness? Shall I trade it in for something more appropriate?"

Mom gave him a huge grin. "Absolutely. It's as plain as the egg on your face."

"Then I'll do it. First thing tomorrow morning."

In spite of himself, Derek felt a little better. This didn't address the deadly ghost problem, but at least he wouldn't have to go to school in a big embarrassing Transport of Shame.

As they all headed upstairs, he thought about his day. He shouldn't be faced with stuff like this. He was only twelve. But here he was, torn between happiness about the new car and fear of two headless ghosts his parents didn't believe in.

If only he could come up with a way to convince them that the Hyde Funeral Home & Used Coffin Outlet was a terrible idea. That they should leave, and soon. Then, with a little luck, he might actually live to see thirteen.

4

The Killer Rabbit

DEREK HURRIED DOWNSTAIRS, LATE FOR BREAKFAST. HE hadn't slept very well, what with all his ghoulish nightmares about wolves and ghosts, sledgehammers and rats. And hats made of underpants.

In the kitchen, he noticed something missing. "Where's Dad?"

"He's gone to buy a new car," Mom answered. "Remember?"

Derek had completely forgotten. Yes! No having to go to a brand new school in an old, yellow Testament to Indignity. Now he'd arrive in style. In a typical, unassuming, unimaginative, one-hundred-percent boring car nobody would ever notice.

He could barely eat his breakfast, squirming in his seat. Derek knew his parents hadn't had a new car in years, scrimping and saving as they did for the big move to Littleburp. This was a great day. The best.

The second a car pulled up outside, he leaped from his kitchen stool and barged through the great hall and out the front door.

He stopped at the porch.

"How do you like it?" Dad threw both arms up in the air as if he were signaling the World's Most Spectacular Touchdown. He stood next to their new car. Large. Shiny. Black.

"You bought a hearse."

"Don't you love it? I love it. Your mom will be over the moon. Isn't it great?"

"You bought a hearse!"

"It's the very latest in vehicular burial transportation. The car dealer said it was previously owned by the Paranormal Pizza Delivery Service. He didn't even call it a hearse. This, my boy, is a Funeral Coach. Not brand new, but pretty new."

"You bought a hearse?"

Mom appeared behind Derek, holding his school backpack. "Oh Honey Bumpkin, it's beautiful! In fact—it's to die for!" She let out a long, hilarious peal of self-delighted laughter.

"And check this out." Dad leaned inside the driver window and pressed the center of the steering wheel. The car's horn blared out a slow, morbid tune: DUN DUN DA-DUN, DUN DA-DUN DA-DUN DA-DUN.

"What's that?"

"That, my boy, is *The Funeral March*, by Frederic Chopin. Pretty classy, huh?"

"Wow."

Mom skipped off the porch and flung herself into Dad's arms. "You continue to amaze me, you incredi-licious man. I think I'll marry you all over again."

Derek winced as she gave Dad a big sloppy kiss. *Gross.*

Dad slipped back into the driver's seat, talking over his shoulder. "Well, what do you say, Derek? Ready to head off to your first day of school?"

"Um… sure. Where do I sit?"

"Oh. Well. About that. Your mother'll want to sit up front, so you need to squat on the floor in the back. Where the coffin goes."

"Of course. Squat in the back. So obvious. I should've guessed."

He opened the large door at the rear and scooted his butt toward the front seats.

Usually, he'd press his nose to the window during the whole enthralling trip to a new school. Not today. Today he lay down flat, well below the windows, and prayed nobody would see him.

That little subterfuge almost failed when his dad stopped at a light next to a long city bus filled with a dozen of the finest citizens of the noble town of Littleburp. Fortunately, they were all staring at their cell phones. Not a single person noticed him.

Unfortunately, things didn't go that well when they pulled up in front of his school. Especially since Derek had forgotten to ask his dad *not* to do the one thing he was sure to do.

"Well, here we are," Dad announced as he stiff-armed the horn to herald their arrival with another blast of the Theme from Chopin's *Funeral March*.

Riding in an actual Funeral Coach suddenly made perfect sense. Because he could have just died. Right then, right there.

He wiggled to the back of the hearse, pulled on the handle and kicked the door open. Tried to ooze out like a blob of hot tar, all the time wishing he were invisible.

"Have a great day at school, Honey." Mom handed over his backpack.

"Knock 'em dead, Sport!" Dad said.

As they drove away with a fading repeat of Chopin's masterpiece, Derek noticed for the first time that his dad had written a cheery message with a bar of soap on the back window: JUST BURIED.

He put his head in his hands.

When he straightened, every kid and parent within three hundred feet quickly turned away as if they hadn't been morbidly fascinated by his strange arrival.

He found himself standing in front of a large brick building with stained white columns, long overdue for a good paint job. The north side of the building ended at the school parking lot, and the south side faced a marshy pond filled with lilies and water reeds.

He took a deep breath and assumed his best don't-give-a-hoot attitude as he slung on his backpack and strode through the large double doors of the Heddy S. Kidd Middle School.

His parents had told him there was no finer seat of learning for a mile in any direction, at least. Much admired by the principal and possibly even a janitor or two, it recently won all kinds of awards. Well, one award: Most Student Requests for Transfer to Another School.

Once inside, Derek breathed more evenly. While he didn't feel exactly normal, at least here he could be overlooked. He headed for the main office and threaded his way through a bunch of kids to the counter.

A prim lady with large round glasses and several yellow pencils stuck in her hair bun gave him an expectant look.

He offered a weak smile. "Hi. I'm Derek Hyde."

"Yes, you are." She grabbed a clipboard and searched the countertop. "Now, where did I put my pencil?"

"It's in your hair."

"That's ridiculous. Why would I put—" She reached up and, feeling the pencil's eraser, grabbed it and held it poised above the clipboard. "Name?"

"I already told you, I'm Derek Hyde and—"

"Of course you are. Got you listed right here. First day. Your homeroom teacher is Mr. Hal Arious, room 107, out this door and to your left. Here's your class schedule. Next!"

He found his homeroom easily enough and slid behind an open desk near the back. A breezy man with freckles and fizzy red hair sailed into the room and plopped down behind his teacher's desk.

A small, brown, cloth-covered box above the whiteboard crackled and filled the space with a painful feedback screech and the morning's P.A. announcement.

Mr. Arious lip-synched the words. Apparently, he'd heard them before.

"Good morning, children. As usual, we begin the day with the school song. Please stand and sing along."

Everybody stood. But no one sang except Mr. Arious, who gave it his enthusiastic best.

" Heddy S. Kidd,

Heddy S. Kidd,

Here's where you'll find us, Heddy S. Kidd.

We couldn't be prouder,

We're so cool,

At Heddy S. Kidd Middle School!"

All the students sat down. The voice on the P.A. system continued, *"Today is Monday, October 26th.*

"Whoever stole Mrs. Wiggleworm's insect collection, please return it before the end of the day. You may have contracted sleeping sickness from the tsetse flies.

"Coach Thangertue has asked all the boys in his gym class to refrain from using their jock straps as slingshots. Especially pointed at the girl's gym class. This is your last warning.

"Principal Throttlebottom would like to personally congratulate all the kids who volunteered for the annual Boy's Bathroom Sanitary Scrubbing Event. Unfortunately, nobody volunteered. Shame on you.

"This concludes today's announcements. Have a great Heddy S. Kidd day."

The school bell rang and Derek checked his schedule. Next class, History. Room 212, Mrs. Julie S. Caesar.

He made it with time to spare. He even had time to notice a familiar face. A disgruntled, white-haired kid, sitting near the back. He'd know that scowl anywhere. Nussbaum. The kid with headless parents. The kid arrested on his front lawn. The kid who hated Derek at first sight. *Great.* Shouldn't he be in Juvenile Hall? Or in a Home for the Wickedly Weird?

Derek found a seat as a plump, gray-haired, bespectacled lady with arms full of books poked her head into the room and asked, "Is this the... um... history class?"

Several students answered in unison, "Yes, Mrs. Caesar."

Relief flooded her face. "Oh, good." She made her way to her desk, dumped the books in a pile and turned to stare at the whiteboard. For a long time.

Finally, one girl in the front with glasses and pigtails raised her hand. "Mrs. Caesar?"

"Oh yes, that's right." She picked up a red marker pen and wrote in script: *Mrs. Caesar.*

She turned to the class. "Now, who can tell me where we left off last time?"

The same girl raised her hand. "You were telling us about when President Jimmy Carter was attacked by a killer rabbit."

"Right. And when was that?"

"1979. April, I think."

"Exactly," the teacher said. "In April 1979, Jimmy Carter went on a solo fishing expedition in... um..."

"Plains, Georgia."

"Yes. And he suddenly noticed... um..."

The girl continued for her. "A swamp rabbit swimming toward him. It was large and wet and made strange hissing noises and gnashed its teeth. Jimmy Carter thought it was planning to climb into the Presidential boat, so he counter-attacked with his oar."

"Why, you tell that so well." Mrs. Caesar put her hand to her forehead. "Now, there was something else I was going to tell you about..."

A small boy in the second row raised his hand. "Could it be when President H. W. Bush upchucked in the lap of the Japanese Prime Minister?"

"No..."

"Or maybe when Vice President Cheney shot a Texas lawyer in the face?"

"No, it was something else..." The teacher meandered to the door, opened it and wandered out.

Some of the students calmly started reading. Others tapped on their cell phones, took selfies and threw pencils at each other. The murmur of voices grew as their attention drifted farther away from the absence of their distracted teacher.

Derek stared at the class. He nudged the girl sitting to his left. "Hey, shouldn't somebody do something?"

"Oh, she's having a bad day. It happens." The girl went back to texting.

"Maybe *you* should do something." Derek wondered who that voice belonged to. He turned around. The Nussbaum kid now wore a kind of sneer. "She looks pretty confused to me," he continued. "You should help her. Unless, of course, you're afraid."

Derek flushed a deep pink as the whole class stared at him. But why should *he* be the one to go after her? He turned back around and scrunched down in his seat, trying to figure out how to disappear through the floor.

"I'm talking to *you*, Home Robber," the Nussbaum kid said. "Coward. Fraidy-cat."

Great. That's all he needed. Bullied on his first day at a new school. Perfect.

"Hey. Clean out your ears, scaredy-chicken."

Of course he was afraid. *Exactly* like a scaredy-chicken, feathers trembling. Who wouldn't be? The minute he stepped out of the room, he'd probably get nabbed for not having a hall pass. Then it's off to the principal's office. And who knows what kind of punishment he'd get?

The sound of a worried hen came from Nussbaum's direction. "Bwaakk...Bwaakk..."

That did it. Derek grabbed his backpack, hurried out of the classroom and ran around a corner in time to see his history teacher strolling out through the school's front door. He caught up with her at the top of the steps.

"Um… Excuse me, Mrs. Caesar?"

She turned and gave him a vacant stare. "No, thank you. Thanks all the same." She continued down the steps.

He rushed to her side and took her arm. "I think you want to go this way, Mrs. Caesar."

"I do?"

"Yes, you do."

He led her back through the tall double doors and down the hall toward the Principal's office. He went up to the prim lady with big glasses who still stood behind the counter, shuffling some papers.

"Hi, remember me?" he asked.

She didn't even glance up. "Of course. You're Colonel Charles A. Lindbergh. Also known as Slim, Lucky Lindy and The Lone Eagle. I'd know you anywhere."

"No, I'm Derek Hyde. I think Mrs. Caesar isn't feeling well. Maybe she should see the school nurse."

The receptionist dropped her papers and peered into his face. "And do you have a hall pass, young man?"

"No, see… I…"

"Then you'd better be getting back to class, don't you think?"

Derek helped Mrs. Caesar to a chair. "You'll be okay. This nice lady will take care of you."

As he headed back to class, the school bell rang. Derek checked his schedule. Next class, Biology. Room 235, Mrs. Wiggleworm.

Now where had he heard that name before?

The Reading Bug
785 Laurel Street
San Carlos, California 94070
(650)591-0100

Date: 02-08-2020
Sale: 408540   Time: 03:31 PM

Derek Hyde Knows Spooky When He Sees It
1947796224   Item Price: $11.99 $11.99

1 Items   Subtotal: $11.99
                          Sales Tax (9.250 %): $1.11
                                         Total: $13.10

                          Credit (Visa) Payment: $13.10

                              Amount Tendered: $13.10
                                  Change Due: $0.00

Printed by: The Bug   Register: CashDrawer2

February 8, 2020 03:31 PM

Thank you for shopping with us!

Return Policy:
14 days with a receipt
/ gift receipt.
All items must be unopened
/ unread /
resellable condition.
Items purchased between
Thanksgiving and
Christmas Eve may be
returned through
January 15th

5

A Knot of Frogs

DEREK NO SOONER FOUND AN EMPTY LAB STATION IN HIS Biology class than two tall boys came stumbling into the room carrying a large clear vat filled with cloudy water and a whole knot of live frogs.

Several of the students hurried to surround this exciting collection of amphibious bog dwellers, tapping on the plastic and impressing each other with small croaking and ribbet-ribbet sounds.

Mrs. Wiggleworm arrived like a tornado, bumping the door open with her backside and spinning into the room as she shed sheets of paper from her armload of tests and homework assignments.

"Class, class, please take your seats."

She dumped her cache on the desk and stood back to survey the damage, grabbed her attendance clipboard and ran her finger down it. Then she gazed around the room until she spotted someone.

"Ah, there you are. Class, we have a new student. His name is... let's see..."

Derek started to stand up as she peered at her clipboard again.

"...Norval Nussbaum."

He sat back down again and looked around the room. There he was, sarcastic scowl, white hair and all. *No way. Not in my biology class, too.*

"Wait, I'm sorry. We have *two* new students today. The other is... Derek Hyde. Say hi to our new arrivals, everybody."

Most of the students responded with mildly enthusiastic expressions of *Hi* and *'S'up.*

A sudden and unexpected shaking and squirming inside the frog vat made Mrs. Wiggleworm jump back with a loud, "Ooo, ick! What's *that?*"

A studious boy with chipmunk cheeks filled her in. "Those are the frogs we're supposed to dissect today. They finally arrived."

The teacher straightened her skirt, reached over and, using only two fingers, slowly lifted the transparent lid. One of the frogs threw himself at it, so she dropped the plastic like a hot Frisbee. She gagged a little, as if she might barf any minute.

"Yes. Well. I suppose we should dive right in. So to speak."

She reached across her desk, shuffled through her papers and pulled out the class Biology book.

"Okay, we'll start with Step One: Pithing of a Frog."

The class laughed, which made her head jerk up. One helpful boy explained, "You said pithing." The boy next to him asked, "Where do they pith? Will they pith on me?"

Mrs. Wiggleworm stared them down with a practiced glare, then read the rest of Step One. "To pith, you insert a pin or knife into the frog's mouth or neck to sever the spinal cord."

The teacher gagged again, then continued. "Step Two is to remove the brain."

A shy girl with braces and bangs raised her hand. "But Mrs. Wiggleworm, won't the frog feel a lot of pain?"

"Well, sure he will. Or *she* will. I won't lie to you, on a scale from *Boring* all the way up to *Please Stop I'll Confess Anything*, this pain is probably off the scale. Especially considering that none of you has any experience as frog killers and you'll probably botch the operation in any case. But don't worry, that's temporary. Trust me: painless once the frog is brainless."

At this, she gagged again, then covered her mouth and barged from the room gasping, "Excuse me, back in a sec..."

The class seemed to be used to this behavior since they all turned to other activities as if they'd been watching TV and the commercials just came on.

Derek wasn't too crazy about what he'd heard so far. He knew students usually dissected frogs in Biology, but it never occurred to him that you start with live frogs.

It didn't seem right.

He thought about their natural habitat. Frogs probably had an awesome life before this. Hanging out in the wetlands. Catching flies with their tongues. Singing to the stars at night. There might even be some deliriously happy frogs in that marshy pond he'd seen at the south end of the school, that—

His thoughts were interrupted by the sense that someone stood over him. He looked up to see Norval, arms crossed, saying, "It's not enough you're in my house and my history class. Now you're in my biology class, too."

He wasn't about to be cowed by a white fright wig with legs. Derek stuck out his chin. "Yeah, what about it?"

"Oh, nothing. But I can't wait to see how you handle cutting up a frog. Think you have the stomach for it?"

"Of course I do," Derek said. "It's only science."

"Sure, but have you heard the noise they make when you're killing them?"

"What?"

"It's pitiful. They kick, they scream, they die. And there's nothing quite like a screaming frog..."

What happened next didn't involve thought. More a pure impulse, raw instinct, a classic knee-jerk reaction.

Derek rose from his seat, stomped to the front of the class, bent down and grabbed the vat with both arms. Heavy, but manageable.

Not one student moved as he struggled out of the classroom and down the hall. The lid fell off and water sloshed over the top, leaving a trail of bubbling puddles in the hallway. But no frogs escaped as he made his way to the half-opened window at the end of the hall.

He balanced the vat on the window ledge and leaned out. The pond that shimmered one floor below lapped at the school wall and seemed deep enough. He wrapped his arms around the vat and poured.

That was the day it rained frogs at Heddy S. Kidd Middle School. Right into the pond. And not a single frog croaked.

As he dropped the vat to the floor, somebody grabbed his arm. He pulled back from the red and bulging face of the one and only Mrs. Wiggleworm.

"I don't suppose you have a hall pass," she said.

Without waiting for an answer, she scooped up the vat and marched him to the Principal's office. She barged through the door marked Private and practically threw him into a chair in front of a large walnut desk.

Behind the desk sat a portly man in a coat and vest, vigorously mining for a booger in his left nostril. He let out a startled snort at the interruption, then leaned forward to inspect the boy so unceremoniously dumped into one of his favorite visitor chairs.

"And whom do we have here?" he asked.

Mrs. Wiggleworm placed the empty vat on his desk. "Allow me to introduce Derek Hyde, a brand new student," she said through clenched teeth. "Derek, I would like to present your principal, Mr. Harvey Throttlebottom."

Principal Throttlebottom raised an eyebrow at his fuming employee. "So. I assume this child has committed some sort of unspeakable crime?"

"Oh, I can speak about it, all right. He only kidnapped a whole vat of live frogs and poured the contents into the pond outside."

"He what?"

"He poured today's classroom assignment into the muddiest, mossiest, stinkiest excuse for a waterhole on campus."

"I see." The principal leaned back in his chair and studied his new prisoner. "And what do you have to say for yourself, young man?"

Derek didn't know quite what to say. Then he remembered the fate that Mrs. Wiggleworm had planned for her proposed Victims of Mass Dissection.

"I had to."

"You *had* to? I think you've confused Need with Want." The principal came out from behind his desk, pulled out a handkerchief, blew his nose and then wiped that same handkerchief all over his face. Mrs. Wiggleworm gagged again.

"I had to. They were about to be murdered by unqualified brain extraction."

"Maybe that should be *your* punishment. What do think, Mrs. Wiggleworm? Is turnabout fair play?"

She must have been overwhelmed by the image of frog brains, since she suddenly turned a clammy green. And threw up all over Derek.

With a hasty, "Excuse me…" she covered her mouth (too late) and sprinted out of the room.

Derek glared at the mess on the front of his shirt and yelled after her, "Hey!"

The principal pulled out his handkerchief to cover his own nose and mouth and uttered a muffled, "Turns out, you're more of a stinker than I thought."

He glowered at Derek, then turned and gazed out of his window for a long minute, humming to himself. Finally, he removed his handkerchief and declared, "I have it. I know how you can make this right."

He grabbed the vat and reached it across to Derek. "Take this and fill it back up with frogs from the pond."

Derek folded his arms—which transferred some of the smelly, icky-feeling upchuck to his sleeves. "No. I won't do it."

Principal Throttlebottom turned a mottled crimson, which slowly faded to his more typical pink. He chewed on a thumbnail for a while, his forehead as wrinkled as curdled milk. Then he lit up.

"What if I promise to give your little webbed friends a reprieve? I believe we can return them to Mr. Toad's Frog & Salamander Supply to get the school's money back. After all, I wouldn't want your conscience to eat away at your insides. Would that work for you?"

Derek mulled this over. "I guess…"

"All right then." He pushed the boy out of his office. "You get out there and gather up thirty frogs and I'll tackle the hard part in here, fixing the paperwork."

The pond was even gunkier than Mrs. Wiggleworm had described. Derek took off his shoes and rolled his pants up as far as he could, but he needn't have bothered. It only took a minute of fruitless lunging for quick-jumping frogs before he was completely soaked. At least this wet activity washed off some of the yuck on his shirt.

By the time he finished, he was covered in mud, with big clumps of smelly algae dripping from his clothes. He even found a frog in his left pocket. He added that to his catch.

Good thing his next class was Phys. Ed. Once he finished returning the frogs, he'd be able to take a long hot shower.

It was a lot easier stealing the frogs in the first place than carrying the refilled vat from the pond up one floor to the office. He managed, though, and even felt a little proud of himself. After all, he'd saved countless lives (well, thirty, at least) and prevailed over a whole school administration.

He placed his catch on the floor in front of the principal's desk.

Throttlebottom looked him up and down before finally speaking. "Well done, Mister Hyde. I think we can consider this matter closed."

"Thanks." An odd reprieve, but Derek wasn't about to complain. He added, "I'm sorry I didn't come to you first."

"Well, live and learn, that's my motto. I'll take these…" the principal lifted the vat in a way that avoided getting his suit wet "…back to the Biology class."

Derek must have heard wrong. "So they can be shipped back, you mean?"

The principal smirked. "Oh, no. These frogs will be executed at dawn, as planned. Well, at tomorrow's Biology class, anyway." He headed out of his office with his prize, adding over his shoulder, "Live and learn."

Derek couldn't move. He'd never felt so betrayed. So helpless. So slimy Later, he stood in the gym shower washing himself and his clothes for a long time, long after the other students had gone off to lunch.

When he finally appeared in the cafeteria, cleaner but sopping wet, everybody had already filled their trays and found their seats.

Derek selected his food and squelched his way between tables, searching for an open chair. He finally found one and headed for it when he noticed—the white-haired Norval Nussbaum.

He looked around for another empty chair. Nothing. This was the only empty seat in the room. He sat down and pretended to be massively preoccupied with his fascinating lunch.

It didn't work.

Norval leaned forward and almost whispered. "Hey, Squirt."

Spit for Luck

DEREK HAD NEVER HAD AN INSTANT ENEMY BEFORE. Now he kept running into him wherever he went.

Norval ran his hand through his white hair and peered at Derek. "Nice move, back there in Biology. You're a frog-rescuing hero. Saved 'em all from a fate worse than death," Norval sneered, then gurgled with nasty laughter. "Actually, that fate *plus* death."

Derek decided to try a civilized conversation. "It wasn't such a great move. Principal Throttlebottom made me recapture all the frogs from the pond. They'll get their brain-ectomies tomorrow."

"Gee, that's too bad. Poor baby." Norval reached across the table to snatch something behind Derek's left ear. He presented him with a tiny, pink plastic rattle and a sarcastic grin.

Derek gave a low whistle. "How did you do that?"

"That's not all I can do." Norval wiggled a finger at the French fries on his plate. One of them started to vibrate, then rose and hovered. He flicked his finger and the fry flew across the table at Derek's face, hitting him in the forehead.

"Hey!"

"Sorry, did my French fry smack you in the head?" He repeated the magic trick and another fry hit Derek on the cheek.

"Cut it out."

"Why, does it bother you?" Norval flicked his finger again and a third fry flew at Derek's chin. "I bet it doesn't bother you as much as I got bothered, being pulled out of the house I was born in. How do you like my house, by the way?"

Derek shrugged, ignoring the fry sliding down his waterlogged shirt. "I like it fine. Freak."

"You think that's freaky? I'll show you freaky." Norval stood up, grabbed all the remaining fries on his plate and heaved them at Derek's face.

Not to be outdone by a complete weirdo, Derek picked up a pickle slice from his own plate and flicked it at Norval's left eye. It looked like a bright green monocle for the second before it fell into his lap.

That did it. They both exploded in a melee of chow-chucking and food-flinging, wildly seizing and turning every edible morsel within reach into a kid-seeking missile.

An eager boy at the next table yelled "Food fight!" and the whole cafeteria joined in the battle. The air was thick with flying pizza slices, mustard-wet hamburgers, soggy sesame seed buns, half-eaten apple slivers, chocolate pudding cups and dripping cartons of juice and milk.

In the middle of this blizzard of generous food sharing, a tall, stern teacher with green glasses and a permanent frown stormed into the cafeteria and shouted, "Cease and Desist!"

The room went silent.

"Okay," she hollered. "What's this all about? Who started it?"

Without a pause, everyone pointed at Derek and Norval, their culpability evident from the lunch morsels plastered all over their hair, faces and clothes. Not to mention the food still in their guilty hands.

"Right. You two, over here." The teacher grabbed each of the boys by a lunch-splattered arm and dragged them off to the principal's office.

Derek went limp, imagining the worst. *Fantastic. I'll probably be sent home for this. On my first day. Shoved through the big front doors with my new arch-enemy. In front of classrooms full of kids. Perfect.*

Marched into the office, Derek winced as Principal Throttlebottom hastily pulled an ear-waxed finger out of his left ear, straightened himself in his large, upholstered chair and cocked his head to one side.

"What's this now? Is that Mister Hyde darkening my doorstep again?" He eyed the teacher. "Ms. Prissynose, is there a problem?"

"A food fight in the cafeteria. Huge. Grub all over the place. And these two started it."

"Hmm. I know Mister Hyde, here." He squinted at Norval. "And who are you?"

"Nussbaum. Norval Nussbaum." He pointed to Derek. "But *he* started it."

"That's a lie!" Derek wrestled his arm away from Ms. Prissynose's grasp. "You started it, and you know it."

The principal shook his head. "Derek, Derek, Derek. Since you've already been in my office more than once today, I think it's pretty clear who the troublemaker might be." He turned to Norval. "You can go."

Norval scowled at Derek, ran a single finger across his neck, spun around and marched from the room.

Derek couldn't believe any of this. *Norval gets off totally free? I'm the only one who gets any blame? Not fair!*

Principal Throttlebottom stood, put his hands behind his back, head bowed as he paced back and forth. "Most unusual. It's been a long time since we've had such a rabble-rouser in our midst. Most uncommon."

He stopped, leaned down to glare into Derek's face, then continued his pacing. "What to do, what to do? We need a really appropriate punishment, something that'll stick with you long after you've left our hallowed halls. Nothing to spit at, but—" He stood up straight. "I have it."

The Principal grabbed Derek by the shoulders, turned him around to face the door and pointed down the hallway. "At the end of that hall is a stairway going down. At the bottom of the stairs, you'll find the Band Room. You'll know it by its tiers, like an amphitheater."

He moved around to his desk and sat down. "I want you to find the brass section. That's the stinky section. You know why? Because that's where the kids with spit valves sit. See, the spit builds up in their instruments, so they open their spit valves to let it out. Right onto the linoleum floors. Lots and lots of spit. Disgusting, really."

He put his elbows on the desk and touched his fingers together. "You will give the floor a thorough cleaning. With this."

He reached into his desk and brought out a toothbrush.

Derek started to speak, but Throttlebottom held up his hand. "Not a word. Not an objection, not a complaint, not a protest. Take the toothbrush to the janitor's closet—that's right outside the band room—and fill a bucket with soapy water. When you're done scrubbing all the spitty areas, you can leave. I'll inspect your work later."

The principal stood. "If it's clean enough, no problem. If not—" Like Norval Nussbaum, he ran a finger across his neck.

No point arguing with Throttlebottom. Derek took the toothbrush, turned on his heel and strode out.

He discovered the janitor's closet all right, complete with a deep concrete sink and shelves of cleaning equipment and solutions. He grabbed a bucket, poured in a pink liquid labeled:

SOPHIE'S SUPER SOLUABLE
SCRUB-A-DUB SOAP (REFILL)

and topped it off with warm water.

In the band room, he wasn't sure which section the brass players used. No instruments on chairs, no sheet music on the music stands. He did notice a tuba in the upper right corner wrapped around a gangly, pony-tailed girl wearing blue jeans and a gray hoody with a unique slogan: "SAYS YOU."

Behind her tuba stood a tall kid. Derek couldn't see who he was at first, until he stepped forward, rubbing his tall forehead. Norval Nussbaum. *Is this guy everywhere?*

Norval glanced at Derek, whispered something to the girl and stepped down the band room tiers. Without a word, he brushed past Derek, almost knocking him over.

The girl extracted herself from her tuba, then turned her focus to the bucket in Derek's left hand and toothbrush in his right. "If you're here for a dentist, he had to rush out. Something about a hippo with an abscess."

"Thanks. I'm trying to figure out where the brass section sits."

"Oh, that. All over the place. The trombone section is over there…" she pointed to three chairs grouped together on the second tier, "…and the trumpet players sit there." She pointed to the third tier. "Next to them, you have the baritone horn and the French horn. (Between us, I think he has a crush on her.) And up here…" she spread both arms out from her own instrument. "…is where the tuba player sits. That's me."

"You play the tuba."

"Sure, why not?"

"Because it's big," Derek said. "And it's bulky. And it's—"

"Not for girls? Yeah, well, that's why."

"Oh. Right. Good reason."

She studied him for a second and then offered, "My name's Prudence."

"I'm Derek. Derek Hyde." He moved up to the trombone area, slid to his knees, dipped his toothbrush in the bucket and started scrubbing.

Prudence laid her tuba on the ground and stepped down the tiers to stand next to him. "It's not easy, you know."

"Tell me about it. This toothbrush is tiny."

"No, I mean playing the tuba."

"Right," Derek said. "That's what I was saying. Too heavy."

"It's not the weight, I can handle that. It's the bullying. How would you like it if everybody called you Tubby the Tuba?"

He glanced up at her, surprised at her friendliness. "Not much."

"Also Prune-face." She sat down, cross-legged. "And Poo-dance, that's the worst."

"That sucks eggs."

"Yeah. Well, what can you do?"

Derek thought about this. "My parents always say if you ignore name-callers, they'll stop."

"Tried that. Doesn't work." She grinned. "I have a better trick. Every time they call me a name, I say something like, 'Haven't you heard? My new nickname is Cool-dance,' or 'You're behind the times. Now they call me Awesome.'"

Derek smiled as he worked. After a while, he put his brush down. "I hope you don't mind my asking, but do you know that kid very well?"

"What kid?" she asked.

"The tall kid with white hair. Are you friends?"

"Oh, him. No, I never saw him before. He was asking for directions to the… uh… to the gym. I guess he's new here."

"Oh." He started scrubbing again.

She leaned closer. "What are you doing, anyway?"

"This is my reward for starting a food fight that I didn't start."

"Oh, I heard about that. An amazing grub grab in the cafeteria. But they said it was started by a new kid. That was you?"

"First day."

"How do you like it so far?"

"Great," Derek said. "Literally great. My History teacher has no short-term memory, my biology teacher thinks frogs are icky and the Principal has no principles."

"You're hilarious." She looked at him more closely. "Hey, are you the kid who stopped Mrs. Caesar from wandering into the street, then rescued a whole bunch of frogs?"

"Yeah, that's me. The last boy scout. I'm off to a great start."

"Sounds to me like you fit right in."

He stopped his work and slouched against a chair. "It wouldn't be so bad if it weren't for that kid you were talking to. He hates my guts. He's the one who started throwing food first, then blamed it all on me."

"Why, what did you do to him?"

"Nothing. I don't even know him. Well, I know *about* him. His name is Norval, and he used to live in the house my parents bought last week. To convert to a funeral home. He got evicted when his mom and dad died."

"Wait. Your parents own a funeral home?"

"Yeah. They're morticians."

She stood up. "Your parents are undertakers? How cool is that?"

"They're really my adoptive parents. I used to be in foster homes until they took me in."

"No way. Sounds like an adventure."

Derek chewed on his lip. "You wouldn't say that if you lived in the Mother of All Spooky Houses like me. You should see my bedroom. Everything's the color of a bat. Stuck in a tar pit. At midnight."

"So—yellow then?"

"Very funny." He returned to his scrubbing. "And that's not all. The most horrible part is the rocking-wolf and two ghosts in the attic." He took a deep breath and shivered. "Norval's decapitated parents."

Prudence snorted. "Sure. And I've got vampires in my basement."

"I'm not joking. There's a secret staircase from my bedroom closet to the attic and when I went up there, a stuffed wolf on rockers growled at me. Later, I discovered the two ghosts. With no heads."

"And you saw this."

"With my own eyes. Totally freaked me out."

Prudence folded her arms. "Why should I believe you?"

"Believe what you want. I'm telling you what happened."

She gave him a skeptical grimace. "Okay, let's say you *think* you're telling the truth. Why would ghosts haunt your house?"

"How do I know? Maybe they died there. And they probably had some unfinished business."

"Sure," She said. "Like maybe their violent deaths, for one thing."

"Yeah, like that."

Prudence brightened. "Or... You said they were headless? Maybe they're looking for their missing brains. Ever think of that?"

He stopped scrubbing and sat back. "Right. With nothing above the collar, they're wildly searching for their thinking ends so they can plop them back on, easy-peasy."

She continued, now on a roll. "Well, maybe. Think about it. They misplaced their heads somehow, and they can't go to their final resting place until they find them. Which means they're doomed to wander through the house, groping around—since they don't have eyes—for all eternity. Or until their heads pop up."

"Pop up?"

"You know what I mean." She sat down again. "You should help them."

He returned to scrubbing, but more furiously. "No way."

"I'm serious. You should locate their noggins. To return to their bodies. Of course, you'd have to find those, too. Any idea where the bodies are buried?"

Derek shuddered. "Don't know, don't care. I always try to take long detours around anything to do with missing heads, or bodies, or ghosts—or funeral homes, for that matter."

She scoffed, "Oh, are we a little bit paranoid?"

"Paranoid? No." He scrubbed harder. "Paranoid means you're crazy. I've got plenty of perfectly sane reasons to be scared."

"Oh, come on. Wouldn't you like to be a kick-butt hero?" she asked.

"What, and get my butt kicked? No thanks."

"I'd be willing to bet a dollar you're braver than that. Like, you were brave enough to rescue Mrs. Caesar. And what about the frogs? That wasn't exactly timid."

"That's something else."

"Why?" She put her hands on her hips. "If you can be brave about that stuff, you can be brave about anything."

"Easy for you to say. You haven't seen where I live."

"Okay, take me there."

"Right. We're supposed to be in school, remember?" He dipped his toothbrush in the bucket. "Besides, I have to finish cleaning all this spit off the floor."

"I meant after school. But you'll never finish with that thing. Wait here, I'll check the janitor's closet."

She rushed from the room and returned with two scrub brushes. "Now I need some way to keep them on."

She stepped into the walk-in band uniform closet, snagged two red cords from the front of a uniform and used them to attach the scrub brushes to her tennis shoes. "Could you throw some water over here?"

Derek grabbed the bucket and sloshed soapy water along the length of the tier. Prudence skated back and forth on the scrub brushes as smoothly as if she were on roller blades. After giving the trombone area a thorough cleaning, she clomped her way up to the next level to attack the trumpet section.

A pear-shaped figure appeared in the doorway accompanied by a bellow. *"What do you think you're doing?"*

Derek dropped his toothbrush and Prudence glided to a stop. They turned to see the familiar and most fabulously rotund silhouette of their beloved principal.

"I asked you a question."

Prudence stared down at her foamy feet. "Um… helping out a new student?"

"Truly? I don't think so."

Derek interrupted. "It's my fault, Principle Throttlebottom. I was complaining about how hard it was to clean the—"

"Silence!" Throttlebottom swaggered into the room. "I can see quite clearly what's going on here." He pointed his finger at Derek. "Not content to commit Heinous Crimes against Frogs and Humanity, you've elected to corrupt your fellow classmates."

"No, but—"

"Quiet! And you—what is your name?"

"Prudence. Um… Prudence Albright."

"And what are you doing out of class?"

"It's my study hall. The teacher said I could come here to practice the tuba since it's so hard to carry home."

"I see." The principal stepped up to the bandleader's podium, held it with both hands and spoke as if he were making an announcement at morning assembly. "You are both suspended for the rest of the day. I'll call your parents to come take you home." He turned to stride from the room.

"Oh, wait, please!" Prudence dropped to the floor to yank the scrub brushes off her shoes. "Derek's parents are picking me up too, I'm supposed to go to his house. My mom and dad are at the… um… Assisted Living Center to visit my Aunt… um… Adnausia."

"And do you have a note from your parents about this?"

"Yes, it's… um… I already handed it in at the office."

"Fine. I'll call the Hydes. You two wait outside on the front steps until they arrive." He stormed from the band room and, without looking back, gave a little wave.

Derek spun around to face Prudence. "Aunt Adnausia?"

"Sure. My favorite aunt." She winked. "Or maybe it was Ambrosia.

2

The Hydes' First Body

DEREK WASN'T EXACTLY TICKLED A BRIGHT SHADE OF PINK at the thought that Prudence would be sharing the World's Most Embarrassing Ride Home in the family hearse. Especially since she found the idea so completely exceptional and totally rad.

As he feared, his dad started playing Chopin's *Funeral March* from over a block away—a performance only slightly more cringe-worthy than the way the big black hearse came to a noisy, brake-screeching halt in front of the school and his dad leaped out to greet him.

"Hi, Sport. I hear your first day was a doozy."

"Hi, Dad. Hi, Mom. Sorry I got into trouble. This is Prudence."

Prudence waved. "Glad to meet you."

As they crawled through the rear door to be driven away, Prudence beamed. "This is so cool. I wish *my* parents had a hearse."

"Good idea," Derek said. "Maybe you could get them to buy ours."

She pursed her lips. "Come on, Mr. Frogcatcher. Where's your sense of adventure? You're the great and amazing Derek Hyde." She blinked twice. "Hey, your name even starts with the sound of the word 'Dare.'"

Derek thought about this. She was right, of course, but he had the perfect come-back. "Yeah, but it ends with 'Ick—Hide.'"

The mansion didn't seem too ominous as they pulled up in the front. Instead of hammering rain, leaves chased each other across the lawn. Instead of thunder and lightning, the afternoon sunlight poured itself down the front of the wooden porch.

Derek wondered if Prudence saw this house as he did. Essentially, creepy. With a whole bunch of weird thrown in, a lot of spooky, some juicy green bits of icky and a large dollop of eww.

But plenty of cobwebs still decorated the corners of every room. Shuttered windows still refused to let in any more light than was absolutely necessary. And the reception area still smelled of badly burnt wood.

Prudence walked through the place transfixed, craning her head to see everything. "This is the best. So great."

"Isn't it though?" Mom cooed. "I find it deli-licious. Gothic Chic. Check out our massive staircase!"

"Now, Pumpkin Patch, don't you go bragging," Dad admonished her. "Speaking of which! We got our first body today. A defunct old gentleman arrived a few hours ago. Our very first customer."

Mom glanced at the Restful Sleep Room. "Of course, the embalming machine wasn't delivered yet, so the corpse is a little stinky…"

"Actually, a *lot* stinky…"

"And oh, my sweet Lord, the flies!"

"…but not to worry," Dad said. "We tripled up on the body bags."

"We put a bag, within a bag, within a bag, within a—"

"I think they get it, Kumquat. Anyway, those bags plus seven bottles of Corpse-Be-Gone air freshener pretty much took care of the problem."

"Um… That's great, Dad. So… We'll be in my room." Derek led the way up the stairs and into his Den of Doom.

As they stepped inside the room, Prudence let out a whispered, "Wow."

"See? Not yellow at all."

"Can't argue about that. About as not-yellow as you can get."

"Wait'll you see the secret stairs to the attic." He opened the closet door and grabbed the ebony coat hanger. As before, the back wall slid open to reveal the wooden steps and dangling light bulb. He pulled the string and stood aside. "Go ahead. I'll protect the rear."

"What do you mean, *go ahead*? How about *you* go ahead and I'll protect *your* rear?"

"That's okay," he said. "I'll stay here. I'm sure you can find the ghosts up there without any help from me."

"Oh no, you don't." She grabbed his arm. "I'm not saying I believe you exactly, but I'm sure as heck not going up those dusty stairs to a creepy old attic all by myself."

"Hey, you'll be fine. I was up there, and I'm still in one piece, aren't I?"

"No, I'd say you're in several pieces. Where's your mojo? Where are the guts you showed all day at school?" She nudged him.

"Hey, I have mojo. I have guts. But I don't want to go up into the attic right now."

"Uh-huh." She nodded sarcastically. "And when do you think you might want to go up?"

"I don't know, maybe Christmas."

"No way." She got behind him and pushed.

"Um…" he said, over his shoulder, "How about you go first?"

"Why should *I* go first? You know the way, after all."

"Yeah," he said. "Up."

As before, the swinging light bulb threw unnerving shadows onto the wall as they crept up the creaky stairs. With a thumping heart, Derek stepped through the trap door and into the attic.

Prudence, right behind him, scratched her head. "Well? Where are they? All I see are some old magazines and a few boxes."

"Didn't you notice the hairy hobby horse in the corner?"

She looked in the direction he pointed. "Wow. That's the stuffed wolf that growls?"

"And snarls, too. I wouldn't get too close."

"Okay. But what about the headless ghosts?"

"You're right, they're not here. Well, I guess we won't see them today. Too bad." He headed for the stairs.

"Oh no, you're not getting off that easy. Let's give it a minute." She walked around the room, leafed through a few magazines, peeked in a box and pulled out a bicycle chain. "I wonder what this is for?"

"Don't ask. That Norval kid was into some weird stuff."

"Oh, I don't know. Lots of boys are into military stuff—" She froze. "Do you smell that?"

He sniffed. "Uh-oh. It's that rotten egg smell. It stank up the place once before, when—" He stopped. The hair rose on the back of his neck.

A putrid mist drifted from the floor, swirling and tumbling in a glob-like mass at first, then slowly taking the horrifying shapes of two headless bodies.

Prudence turned a green-tinted shade of white.

Once the ghastly couple appeared whole, though weirdly transparent, they moved forward with flailing arms.

This time, Derek wasn't exactly nailed to the floor. His legs sprinted him across the attic, through the trapdoor, down the steps and out of the closet without a conscious thought.

Prudence came down much slower, with a pensive look on her face.

"Did you *see* that?" he heaved between gasps, all bent over. Then he noticed the tears in her eyes. "Are you okay?"

She shook her head. "It's sad…"

"But—but— Weren't you afraid?"

She gave him a blank look. "Afraid? No… Sorry for them, though. They lost their heads, after all…" She sat down on the floor. "By the way, were you planning to leave me up there?"

"Me? No, I had a bout of… um… Restless Leg Syndrome. Had to walk it off."

"Don't you mean *run* it off?"

He sat down next to her. "Look, I'm sorry, but I get totally scared by all this freaky stuff, you can't imagine."

"Oh, I don't know," she said. "I have a pretty good imagination."

"Really, I can't stand it. I've even been thinking of hitting the road."

Prudence's head went back. "What? Run away? Uhn-uhn. That's not okay."

"Why not?"

"Well, for one thing, you're in—what, seventh grade?"

"Yeah, but—"

She rested her palms on the floor behind her and leaned back. "And for another thing, you'd be leaving your parents here alone to deal with the ghosts by themselves."

"I know, but—"

"And they adopted you. They seem to honestly care about you. They'd be crushed if you disappeared." Prudence sat up straight. "Hey, we should tell them what we saw."

Derek shook his head. "I already tried that, right after the wolf growled at me the first time. They even went up there, but didn't see anything."

"But this time you have a witness. Me. Come on."

He followed her to the grand staircase mumbling, "Maybe I could convince them we should *all* leave. The whole Hyde family. Gone."

"That'd be pretty hard. Did you not notice how much they love this place? Especially your mom."

"Well, sure they do, *now*. But—what if bad things started to happen? Like spooky things."

As they reached the bottom landing, the burnt smell from the reception area gave his words extra meaning.

Prudence tilted her head. "What kind of spooky things?"

Derek thought about this. "For example, what if that body that arrived today suddenly sat up in its coffin? That would really scare them, right?"

"I don't think you can bend a body after it's been dead a while, 'cause—rigor mortis. You know, the thing that makes stiffs… well, stiff."

"Oh, right. Okay, how about this? What if weird things start happening all over the funeral home, and they flunk their city inspection, so they lose their mortician's license?"

Prudence paused at the bottom of the stairs. "How?"

"I don't know. Maybe bodies start disappearing. Or the embalming fluid gets replaced with orange juice."

She looked at him sideways. "Or you change the funeral music to bee-bop. Or you replace the flowers with dead weeds."

"There you go. Now you're thinking."

"No, I'm not. I'm being ironic."

"You are?"

Prudence stopped him before they walked into the kitchen. "Derek. Your parents are morticians. That's their career. That's what they love to do. Do you honestly mean you'd scuttle their funeral home? Would you really do that to them?"

He shuffled his feet. "No, I guess not."

"You can't sabotage their dreams. That's not you."

"How do you know what's me? We just met."

"And I already know a lot about you." She cupped her hand on her chin. "I know you were kind to Mrs. Caesar."

"Sure, but—"

"And you cared enough about a bunch of frogs to try to save them from certain death."

"I know, but—"

"So you can't convince me that you care more about teachers and frogs than you do about your own parents, even if you're adopted. *Especially* if you're adopted."

Derek knew when he was stumped. "Okay, you got me. I won't sabotage the funeral home. But I can't live here with ghosts in the attic."

"Right. That's why we have to find their heads."

Mom's Meat Cleaver

S SCARY THINGS GO, DEREK COULDN'T IMAGINE ANYTHING more frightening than snarling wolves and headless, gurgling ghosts in his attic.

Well, okay, he might be more scared madly swimming away from a great white shark with a toothache. And a bad case of barnacle belly.

And all right, it's true that he'd be more terrified by a giant hairy bigfoot with dripping fangs. If it roared in his face. And smelled like his school gym locker.

But that's about it.

Derek and Prudence found his mom and dad sitting at the kitchen island, going over plans for the house overhaul.

"Mom, Dad. Wait'll I tell you. I saw the ghosts again. Prudence saw them, too."

Prudence agreed. "It's true, Mr. and Mrs. Hyde. They had see-through bodies."

"With blood-soaked clothes." Derek pulled at his own shirt.

"And stumps where their heads should have been."

"And they shuffled when they walked." Derek did an impression with his arms stretched out, then concluded with a breathless, "We were lucky to escape!"

Mom's face glowed. "That sounds phantasma-gorically amazing. How phenomenal is that?" She turned to Prudence. "And you honestly think they're real?"

Dad interrupted. "Because remember, we were up there in the attic ourselves, and we didn't spy a single spook."

Mom wiggled on her stool. "Which is not to say we don't believe you—"

"No, of course not. If you say you saw something, then by Jove, you saw something. But we'll have to figure out what it is." Dad tapped his chin, squinting at the window.

Mom swept the house plans from the counter and jumped up to stir an old copper pot. The smell of chocolate-cabbage soup wafted through the room.

Prudence nodded. "It's really true. We definitely saw them; I can back up Derek's story one hundred percent. They're up there, honest."

Dad shoved his stool back, the metal legs squealing on the tiles. "Then of course, I'll have to go investigate."

Mom jumped up and stood next to him. "And me, too."

"No, Sweetheart, you should stay to watch over the kids. In case the ghosts come down here." He gave her a sly wink.

Derek put his hands in his pockets and stared at the floor. *They can't go. It's suicide.* "Dad, the more I think about it… Maybe neither of you should go up there. It's not safe."

"Hey, champ, it'll be okay. I'll get the sledgehammer first."

Mom kissed Dad on the cheek. "Good idea, my handsome gorilla. Careful not to make any more holes in the walls."

"That won't help, Dad. They're transparent. The sledgehammer would go right through them."

"Ah, but I'll have the element of surprise."

"Uh… That makes no sense," Derek said.

His dad took a breath. "Of course, what am I thinking?" He slapped his hand to his forehead. "You should come with me."

Derek waved his hands in front of him. "No... that's okay."

"Right. Sledgehammer it is then. Wish me luck!"

"Are you sure you'll be okay, Honey-bumpkins?" Mom rummaged through the knife drawer and pulled out a huge, stainless-steel meat cleaver. "Maybe you should be better armed."

Dad stood taller and gave them all a brave smirk. "I'll be fine. Don't worry about me. You keep that shiny weapon, in case they come down here."

Dad clomped up the staircase as Mom prowled around the kitchen like an over-confident ninja, throwing the meat cleaver from hand to hand and flipping it like a pancake.

She'll lose a few fingers if she keeps that up. Derek rushed over and surprised himself by managing to catch the handle of the flying blade in mid-air. He gave a deep sigh. "Mom, don't you think it'd be better to keep this out of sight? We don't want to irritate the ghosts."

"What a smart boy you are. We'll try charm first. And we'll only use violence as a last resort."

"Um... right." He put the knife back in its drawer.

Mom sniffed the air, then leaned forward to smell Derek's breath. "Did you burp?"

"Mom..." Derek tossed his head toward Prudence.

She got the message at once. "Oh, I'm sorry dear, thoughtless of me." Then she sniffed the air again and stared at Derek's pants. "Did you fart?"

"Mom!"

"Oh sorry, Honey. It's just... don't you smell that? It's like an old mud wrestler crawled into a dirty diaper hamper and died. About a week ago."

Derek and Prudence both caught a whiff. The rotten egg smell. That meant the ghosts could be nearby...

This time, no mist rose from the floor. Instead, two figures shuffled right through the wall, arms out and fumbling as they groped their way toward the kitchen island.

With wide eyes and liquefied legs, the three witnesses slowly backed away. Derek grabbed his jaw with both hands to calm his chattering teeth.

Mom jumped in front of the kids, whispering, "Don't pay them any attention. It might go to their heads."

"But they don't have any..." Derek started to say.

"I got this." Mom put on a slightly plastic smile and turned to the ghosts. "Hello, you two. Welcome to our kitchen. I guess it must be pretty lonely up there in the attic. Would you like some cookies and milk? It'll kill you good."

"What?" Derek and Prudence both asked.

"*Do* you good. It'll *do* you good. Yummy!"

Derek was about to mention that being faceless could make the cookie-eating thing a little tough, but the ghosts didn't show any signs they heard a thing. They kept lumbering forward, wading waist high through the kitchen island as if it were nothing but a deep stream of clear water. They left a trail of green plasma that disappeared as they continued across the kitchen and out through the opposite wall.

Nobody spoke for a full minute after they'd gone. They all simply stared.

Dad returned from upstairs with a big boyish grin. He carried a cardboard box and clutched his sledgehammer under one arm. "Couldn't see any apparitions, but I brought down the box of Halloween decorations. Anybody want to help me dress up the house?"

Mom gazed at him without a hint of recognition. "Hah?"

Dad's smile disappeared. "Poopikins? Are you okay?"

Mom slowly nodded, then stuttered, "They... they... walked through the wall. They... stumbled right across here and back out again through the opposite wall."

"They didn't see us at all," Prudence added.

Mom gave Prudence a kind look. "Of course not, dear, they don't have any eyes. Or heads to hold them in, for that matter."

Derek chimed in. "It's true, Dad. And they didn't hear us, either."

"Which was too bad," Mom added, plopping onto a kitchen stool. "I offered them cookies. And milk."

"Which they can't eat anyway," Derek reminded her.

Dad frowned, delivering a considerable helping of doubt. Then he laughed. "You're pulling my leg, right? You all planned this story while I was upstairs."

"No, Dad, they came right through here, honest."

"The ghosts? Both of them? How exciting. Did you get their autographs?"

Prudence stepped from behind the kitchen island. "Really, Mr. Hyde, we're not kidding."

Dad glanced from face to face, obviously looking for some hint that this was all a cooked-up tale. Then he slowly eased the cardboard box and sledgehammer onto the kitchen counter.

"This is not good." He paced around the room. "What if they show up in our funeral home while we're meeting with some poor grieving widow? No, this won't do. This is not good at all."

Derek lit up. "Yeah, maybe we should move out. I bet you could find another, much better place to start a funeral home. In another town. Far away."

Prudence quietly kicked him in the shin.

Mom put on a more cheerful expression. "Oh, I don't know. Maybe this could bring us a bunch of new customers."

Derek's head jerked around. "Excuse me?"

"I mean when word gets out. You know what they say, *there's no such thing as bad publicity*."

Dad squeezed the back of his neck. "Honey, I'm not sure that applies in this case."

"But honestly," she continued. "Think about it. If you had to choose between a regular funeral home or one that's actually *haunted*, wouldn't you pick the more interesting choice?"

"No," everyone answered at once.

Mom's shoulders slumped. "Well, it was a thought."

She wandered across the room and idly knocked on the wall. "Why do you suppose they're haunting us in the first place?"

Dad put up one finger. "It's usually some unfinished business, isn't it? Maybe some wrong they did that they have to undo. Or maybe it's some revenge they need to exact on somebody before they can go to their final rest."

"Derek and I have a theory."

Derek raised his eyebrows at Prudence. "We do?"

"Sure," she said. "We talked about this. About their missing heads, remember?"

"Oh, yeah." He turned to his parents. "We thought maybe it could be something really simple. Like they're on a quest for their noggins."

Mom rubbed her temples. "But how can they do that? Without heads, they'd die. Wouldn't they?"

"Um... They're already dead, so..."

"Of course, what was I thinking? You might be right. They're only feeling around for a missing body part. A *really critical* body part."

Dad sat on a stool. "I'm sorry I wasn't here to see it. Weren't you all scared?"

"It was actually pretty thrilling," Mom admitted as she rummaged through the cardboard box on the counter. "What's all this?"

He puffed up his chest. "It's those creepy decorations you found in the attic, remember? I thought we could spruce the place up a bit."

Mom clapped. "What a good idea. It's not long until Halloween now. What do you think, Prudence, want to help?"

"I'd love to, Mrs. Hyde, but I have to get home."

"That's okay, maybe we could postpone it till Saturday. Can you come over then?"

"Sure."

"In fact, we could use Saturday to prepare for our first annual Halloween party. Much more exciting than a housewarming, don't you think? Derek, you could invite all your friends."

"Thanks, Mom, I'd rather die."

"Well, that's something everybody should do at least once in their life."

"Besides," Derek said. "I don't have any friends yet."

"You have me," Prudence offered. Her lips curled into a mischievous smile as she added with a twinkle, "And there's always Norval Nussbaum…"

"No way," Derek blurted, then caught sight of Prudence's grin. "Nice, good one."

"Thanks." She brightened. "I know what, I could make a big general invitation, that we could post on the school bulletin board. That would work, wouldn't it?"

He ran his hand through his hair. "I'm not sure. A Halloween party in our haunted mansion? Sounds like a recipe for a complete disaster."

Mom shook her head. "No, it'll be a blast. After they see our mansion, you'll become the most popular kid at school. And we'll get free publicity for the funeral home. Win-win."

"Win-win?" Derek hiked an eyebrow.

"Of course. And your father and I are the world's best hosts."

Dad put his hand up in the air. "Sign me up."

Mom slapped his accidental high-five. "Sure. I can dress up as a wicked old witch. Your dad can be the husband."

"Honey, I don't think witches have husbands. I've never heard of one, have you?"

"Of course they have husbands. At least I think they do." Mom set her jaw. "And if not, they should. They deserve to be as happy as the next person. Right?"

"Of course," Dad said. "Right. Silly me."

Prudence nodded. "I can totally imagine that, Mrs. Hyde. You two make a wonderful witch and witch's husband."

"Thank you, dear."

Dad pulled on his left earlobe. "What's the outfit for a witch's husband?"

"Don't worry about that. We'll figure something out. Now Prudence, do you need a ride home?"

Prudence shook her head. "Oh no, please don't bother. I live only a few blocks away. I can… um… I can walk home."

They saw her to the front door.

"Thanks so much for having me over Mrs. Hyde, Mr. Hyde." She stepped onto the porch, then whispered to Derek, "I'll see you Saturday. We'll find those heads."

They waved as she tripped down the lawn and onto the sidewalk. She waved back.

As she disappeared around the corner, Mom murmured to Derek, "I like that girl. She's smart. And nice. She could be your girlfriend."

"Mom. I'm only twelve. And I think she's older than me, anyway."

"Still…

9

The Painter's Vision

OMPARED WITH HIS FIRST DAY AT HEDDY S. KIDD MIDDLE School, the rest of Derek's week seemed almost tame.

Of course, the teachers will never ever forget that Wednesday when Norval ambushed Derek in the hallway between classes—after which Derek stood up in assembly to demand why school lockers didn't have safety releases on the inside. Or at least a night light.

And then there was Derek's unfortunate incident in Ms. Dotty Latrine's Language Lab when he accidentally called his teacher Ms. Potty Sardine, and it spread all over the whole school. Principal Throttlebottom called it The End of Humanity and Polite Discourse as We Knew It.

Yep, things could have been a lot worse. After all, Derek did make it all the way to Saturday.

The better news was that the moving van finally arrived with all their furniture and other-worldly goods. At last Derek could snooze in his own bed. Or rather, on his own mattress. Which he dragged into the hallway every night to sleep outside his scary room.

He actually hummed to himself as he showed up for breakfast in their newly decked-out dining room, now complete with thick oaken table and chairs, hand-hewn sideboard and medieval chandelier with a natural rust finish. Hey, any mealtime décor was better than having dinner on top of a coffin.

Mom stopped pouring tea from a pink, pig-shaped teapot for long enough to greet Derek with a gigantic grin.

Dad waved. "Happy Saturday, sport!"

"Good morning, my sweet son. Did you sleep well?"

"Um… sure. It only took me a couple of hours to nod off this time."

Dad put down his fork. "Glad to hear it, champ. Pull up a chair. We'd like your opinion. Your mom and I have been talking over all the things we could do to promote the funeral home."

Derek sat down and helped himself to a double serving of marinated monkfish.

Dad burped, then wiped his mouth with his napkin. "The problem is, we're not getting the customers we need."

Mom swallowed her food. "I don't understand what's wrong with this town. Doesn't anybody ever die around here?"

"Don't worry, Lambikens. We'll get some more customers soon. We need to jazz up our offering, is all, to make it irresistible. A compulsion, even."

Mom sat up straight. "Hey, I have an idea. Maybe we could offer a special two-for-one sale on funerals."

"There you go. That's thinking outside the box." Dad took a sip of bug juice. "Or—how about this? How about if we advertise for a band to play snappy tunes at our funerals? With stage pyrotechnics?"

Mom nodded. "Or we could shoot off fireworks at night like they do at Disneyland."

"Or—here's a thought. We could visit all the rest homes in town to schmooze with the old rotting senior citizens who're about to die—"

Derek grimaced. "Why don't you invite a bunch of ambulance drivers over for tea? Then you could convince them to talk up the funeral home every time they have to rush a victim to the hospital."

"Good one, son," his dad stood up and clapped him on the back. "And to seal the deal, in the hospital we could put up glossy pictures of dead people all nicely made up, to show what great makeup artists we are. We can even add a nice slogan. Something like, *The Hyde Funeral Home takes years off your face.*"

"What an absolutely dee-vine solution," Mom enthused. "Well, I feel optimal-mystic all over again."

She stood and started clearing the breakfast dishes. "By the way, Derek, wasn't your girlfriend Prudence coming over this morning?"

"She's *not* my girlfriend," Derek protested. "She's only a friend."

"Of course she is, dear. My mistake." She flashed Dad a smile.

Derek stood to clear his own part of the table when a horrific shriek filled the house. He almost dropped his plate. "What was that?"

"Isn't it wonderful? Your father installed a special Halloween doorbell."

"Our doorbell is a terrified scream?"

"For Halloween," she said. "I love it. Shouldn't you answer the door?"

"It's probably Prudence, sport," Dad suggested. "Don't keep her waiting."

Derek held in a sigh as he headed for the front door. He opened it to a cheerful, pony-tailed Prudence, complete with faded overalls, two paint rollers under one arm and a can of Wild Blue Yonder paint in each hand.

"'S'up, Derek?"

"Hi, Prudence. Just finished breakfast. What's that?"

"Paint. For your bedroom."

"Oh. Right."

"Where should I put it?" She looked around.

"My room, I guess."

"Oh, hey. You got your furniture." She pointed to one of the paint cans at the red velvet couch, distressed Louis XIV desk and odd assortment of fancy display coffins all nicely arranged in the middle of the main hall.

"Yeah, this is the reception room now."

Prudence smiled. "Cool. Show me the rest."

Derek ran a hand through his hair. "Well, the thing is, I never go into the chapel or the embalming room…"

"Come on, scaredy-cat. I want to see."

Derek shifted uncomfortably and bit the nail of his left thumb. "No. You should say hi to my mom and dad instead."

Prudence deposited the cans and roller next to the staircase. "Sure."

As they walked into the kitchen, Derek thought—not for the first time—of the phrase, "merry morticians." As they did every Halloween, his parents wielded menacing knives in front of large, fresh pumpkins, locked in a friendly race to see who could carve the most revolting face the fastest.

"Hi, Mr. Hyde. Mrs. Hyde. I love your doorbell scream."

Dad waved his knife. "Hi there, Prudence old girl."

"Prudence, what a dear," Mom said. "Have you come over to help with the Halloween decorations? We even have jack-o-lanterns. Almost."

"I'd love to pitch in. But would it be okay if I help Derek to paint his room first? I brought supplies."

Mom knitted her brow. "You know how to paint? Aren't you a little young for that?"

"Oh, no. I'm thirteen. My parents always let me do my own room. I've done it in three colors already."

"Well, aren't you talented," she said. "Of course you can. Do you need anything from us? Drop cloths? A stepladder?"

"Both would be great. But first, Derek's taking me on a tour of your funeral home."

Derek's eyes darted left and right. *What is she talking about?* "I am?"

"Yes, you are." She pushed him out of the kitchen.

He led the way to the chapel, shaking his head.

"This used to be the drawing room." He pointed out the podium next to the organ and the one display coffin at the head of seven rows of chairs. "Now it's a chapel for funerals. Mom and Dad are even thinking of replacing that window with the stained glass from their bedroom."

"Nice."

Derek tried not to tremble as he moved to what used to be the library. He opened the door. Which creaked.

Prudence pinched her nose. "It sure smells funny in here."

"The embalming machine arrived a few days ago. You're smelling the embalming fluid. My dad named this the Restful Sleep Room." He shuddered.

Prudence scanned the space for any leftover cadavers, but the room only revealed metal slabs and body drawers. "So this is where they prepare the bodies. It's kind of spooky."

"Tell me about it." Derek headed for the door. "Well, you've seen everything. Let's go."

"Wait a minute. I want to see inside a body drawer."

"They're empty. Nothing inside. No body. Nada."

"What a Nervous Nellie you are." She strode over to the drawers and pulled on the first handle.

Derek took in a sharp intake of breath, then relaxed. The drawer was empty. "Okay, you've seen it. Let's go."

"Wow. You've got it bad, I have to give that to you."

In the main hall, Prudence grabbed her paint and rollers and followed Derek up the stairway. "Have you given any more thought to your ghostly visitors?"

Derek had thought of little else. "They're not visiting. They actually live here."

"If you call that living…" she mumbled.

In the bedroom, Mom had already deposited the stepladder and some drop cloths. Prudence and Derek got to work right away, swabbing swaths of wet blue patches all over the midnight-shaded space.

Derek began to feel for the first time that this could actually be his room. *Not bad. Now if this impressive new space could just lose a headless ghost or two...*

He smiled at Prudence. "It's better already. Thanks for suggesting we do this. And for the paint."

Prudence used one of the black curtains to wipe a smear of paint from the floor. "It's fun."

It took a couple of hours, but the finished product was truly—blue. Blue, blue, blue. Everywhere blue. Derek wondered if they might have overdone it.

"It's kind of overwhelming."

"It's happy. Like the sky. Now it needs to dry." She put down her roller. "Want to take a break? We could visit the cemetery."

Derek snorted. "Don't call it a cemetery. Call it what it is. A graveyard. Because it has graves. And gravestones. With gray, dead bodies underneath."

"Okay. Want to visit the graveyard?"

"No way, definitely not. Why would I want to do that? Besides, we have to help with the Halloween decorations."

"We can help out after. I really want to see the gravestones."

"Because?"

"Because we need to find the spot where they buried the Nussbaums. It must be in the graveyard next door, right?"

Derek glanced over his shoulder at his window. "Oh. Right."

"So. If we want to reunite their heads with their bodies, we need to know one thing. Where their bodies are."

Derek disagreed. "*Two* things. We don't know where their heads are, either."

"First things first. Come on."

She led the way downstairs and out the front door.

Derek wasn't exactly dragged into the graveyard, but he didn't leap there like an overexcited gazelle, either. He simply lagged behind. Even with the sun lighting up the morning mist, the graveyard oozed with creepiness and a strange silence—a definite lack of songbirds and traffic noise.

Prudence hurried down the pathway, past the scraggly boxwoods and gaunt, leafless maples, almost as if she knew exactly where to go.

At last she stopped by a pair of headstones accessorized with stone gargoyles, frowning, their chins in their hands. She waved to Derek. "Come on, lazy butt, I think this is it."

Derek caught up with her.

On the first stone, someone had commissioned the chiseled wisdom of some pretty distinctive epitaphs, delivered as if written by the deceased:

The second stone presented a much shorter message.

Derek wondered who could have written such curious parting words. Probably some weird relative. With a unique sense of humor.

An old weather-beaten comforter, large and green but with several holes, covered both graves as if to tuck the parents in for the night. Was his nemesis Norval responsible? Seemed unlikely.

"Okay," he said. "We've found their resting place. Let's go."

Prudence stood at the foot of the graves with a distant, wistful look on her face. Absentmindedly she murmured, "What's your hurry? We need to figure things out."

"Like what?"

She turned to Derek. "Well, for starters, how do we join the heads with their bodies? Assuming we find the heads, of course. I'm thinking we'll have to dig the bodies up, then put the heads in the coffins…"

"Excuse me?"

Prudence gestured at the grave. "Heads. In coffins. How else can we return their missing property?"

"I don't know," he said. "I thought we could leave them next to the gravestones…"

"That won't work. The heads would be dragged off by jackals."

Derek shook his head. "Littleburp doesn't have any jackals."

"Rats, then." She put her chin in her hand and gave the area a studied look. "No, we have to put the heads back where they belong."

Derek felt a chill and stepped away from the gravestones. "You mean, we have to dig up the—"

"Bodies. Exactly. But first, we have to figure out where the heads are. Have you given this any thought? Like, why weren't the heads found the day of the explosion?"

"I don't know. You'd think the skulls would be discovered in the rubble after the fire was put out. Unless they were pulverized by the blast."

Prudence shook her head. "I don't see how that's possible since the bodies came through it all okay. No, I think the heads were stolen."

"Wait, what?"

"Stolen. Lifted. Pinched. Ripped off."

"Impossible," he said. "Who would do that? And why?"

"Ah, two more pretty good questions." She scratched her right temple. "I wonder…"

10

Deep in the Dungeon

BACK AT THE HOUSE, THE DOORBELL SCREAMED AGAIN and Derek's mom surprised them at the front door, returned from a quick visit to Harry's Horrendous House of Mask & Magic.

"Sorry, I forgot my key." Mom stopped fumbling in her purse. "Isn't it a great day? It's absolutely outdoor-able!"

"Hi, Mom. Been shopping?"

"*I'll* say. I have goodies. And look, I found this shopping cart. It was left there, abandoned, right outside a grocery store."

On the back of the cart's child seat were the words:

PROPERTY OF PIGGLY WIGGLY

She worked her cart into the reception room, then happily trotted out her new additions to Norval's Halloween box: a large cauldron made of black paper mâché (complete with plastic bags of lizard tongues and eyes of newt), a dripping candelabra and a singularly spine-chilling collection of spiders, cobwebs, bats and skeletons. Plus, a set of Texas Chain Saw Massacre greeting cards.

"We can repurpose these as invitations to your Halloween party," Mom said. "What do you think?"

"Awesome." Derek tried for cheery.

Prudence shifted through the loot. "This stuff is stunning, Mrs. Hyde. And so right for your mansion."

Mom visibly brightened and flashed a toothy smile. "Well, okay then. You kids go for it. You can put things wherever you like." She tripped off to the kitchen, yelling, "Ja-aack. I'm ba-aack. Want to help me drag some coffins onto the front lawn?"

Prudence gathered up an armload of decorations and turned to Derek. "Let's start in the embalming room."

"You mean the Restful Sleep Room," Derek said. "Let's not."

She dropped her decorations back onto the floor. "Derek, what's with you? And don't say it's my imagination. You're way more afraid of this funeral home than I'd expect. You just have to live here with a few pesky ghosts."

"Am not."

"Are too. What's up with that? It's not like they're brain-chomping zombies. They've never actually hurt anybody. They only fumble around."

"Yeah, but..."

Prudence picked up the decorations and lined them up on the bottom step of the staircase. "Oh, I know. Your mother was scared spitless by a slasher movie right before you were born."

"It's nothing like that."

"Well then, what? Why are you so paranoid?"

He dug his toe into the carpet and gazed up the stairs. "I'm not paranoid, not exactly. Maybe a little freaked out..."

"Because..."

"Well, if you have to know, my original parents were killed in a pretty gruesome attack by a serial killer clown. I don't like to talk about it much." He glanced at Prudence to see if she was buying this.

Prudence peered at him sideways, wrinkling her nose. "Come on, I'm not swallowing that. You've been bingeing on horror movies, admit it."

"No, it's true. I was in third grade. They were on their way to my school gym to put socks on all the donkeys for a game of donkey basketball, when suddenly—"

"Wait. Now I *know* this is a load of cow pies. Socks on donkeys?"

"Sure." Derek took a breath and continued, "So their hooves don't scratch up the hardwood floors. Anyway, they—"

"Hooves? Hardwood floors?"

"Try to keep up," He humphed. "They were halfway there when they were pulled over by a cop car. Only it wasn't a cop car. Turns out, it was a clown car."

"A clown car."

"Right. And while they were sitting there, rummaging through their glove box for car registration, this dude dressed up as a clown stepped out, slapped a policeman's hat on top of his fright wig and flopped over to the driver-side window."

"Flopped over?"

"On account of his big clown shoes."

"Of course," she said. "Floppy shoes."

"Only he didn't ask for their license and registration. He… well, he… I can't talk about what happened then. You wouldn't be able to look. It was horrible."

"Uh-huh. And how do you know all these details, if both your parents were killed?"

Derek's eyes defocused. "Oh, um… Because the whole thing was witnessed by a…"

"By what?" she asked. "By a Homeless guy?"

"Uh—right. A homeless guy."

"With a cell phone, of course. Who caught it all on video."

"Right."

"Which you watched."

"Right."

"Wait—do you smell that?" She sniffed the air. "Oh, I know. It's your liar-liar-pants-on-fire."

He gave her a sheepish smile. "Okay, I was just kidding. But it's a pretty good story, don't you think?"

She gathered up the decorations from the stairs and smiled back. "You really had me going there—for about ten nanoseconds." She handed him a bunch of big hairy spiders. "Here. These'll be great in the chapel. I'll do the cobwebs."

They Halloween-afied the whole funeral home in less than an hour. Even the Restful Sleep Room, despite Derek's protests that no Halloween guests would ever have a reason to go in there.

Prudence surveyed their work. "You know what? We totally rock. Everything looks spectacular. And now we're free to hunt for some missing cadaver heads."

"Sure." Derek scanned the room. "But where?"

"I don't know. Let's comb through the whole mansion, top to bottom."

"Well, we've already been in the attic, so..."

She sighed. "Okay, bottom to top. Do you have a basement?"

He thought about the night his dad discovered the sledgehammer. "Sort of."

"A cellar?" Prudence snapped her fingers. "Oh, of course. You have a wine cellar."

"Not exactly. Dad calls it a dungeon."

"You have a dungeon?"

"According to my dad."

Prudence hopped from one foot to the other. "Awesome. Let's go."

At the dungeon entrance, Derek put his hand on the doorknob and chanted supportive phrases to himself. Product slogans like "Just Do It" and "Because You're Worth It" swam in his head. But those familiar earworms were soon replaced by "Melts in Your Mouth, Not in Your Hands" and "Got Milk?" So confusing.

He slapped the thoughts out of his head. Then he opened the door and stuck his hand inside to grope around for a light switch. All he felt was a cold rock wall. Fantastic. The open door shot a single shaft of yellow light down the spooky stone stairway.

Derek decided to go first this time. He'd had more than enough of Prudence ragging on him about being so afraid.

She came right behind, so close she almost pushed him. He jumped a little as she whispered, "This is scary. Aren't you scared?"

He turned around to glare at her. "Really? After beating me up for being paranoid, those are the words of encouragement you want to hiss in my ear right now?"

"Sorry."

The dungeon stairs dropped down much farther than he expected, following a long curve in the wall. By the time they neared the bottom, light from the door above shone fainter than a handful of glowworms. He swallowed hard.

Every impulse roared at him to head back upstairs, but he squared his shoulders and kept going. After all, what was there to be so nervous about? Only the distinct probability that they might run into two stumbling spirits without faces, that's all.

On the last step, he squinted into the darkness, barely able to make out a set of wooden shelves filled with old garden tools: rusted hedge clippers, a trowel, a couple of short shovels, an old hoe and a broken-toothed saw.

Prudence put her hand on his arm. "Do you hear that?"

"What?"

"Dripping water."

He touched the wall and shivered at the mossy dampness. "I guess there's seepage. Watch your step."

An unlit torch, as if from a Frankenstein movie, stuck out from a hole in the far wall.

Derek tried to make his voice firm. "I don't suppose you have a match."

"Not me. What's up on that ledge?"

How did Prudence see it in the dark? But she was right, a dusty old box of matches peeked out from a small alcove barely within reach. He nabbed it and struck one, applying the tiny flame to the torch. Soon the smoldering stick sizzled into a halfhearted flame that filled the dungeon's gloom with an ominous shadow dance.

Not exactly the atmosphere he needed right now.

He stood on tiptoes to yank the torch from the hole in the wall. Not as easy as he expected. He seized it with both hands and even lifted his whole body off the floor trying to pull it out. The torch finally gave way.

So did the stone wall.

With a creak and a moan, six square feet of gray masonry pulled back like a barn door to reveal a long, gloomy corridor.

Prudence gulped. "It's a secret passageway."

"Ya think?"

"Well, yeah."

Derek held the sputtering torch high and inched forward, Prudence at his side. After a few steps, she reached into her jeans pocket, pulled out her phone and turned on the flashlight feature.

"Why didn't you tell me you had that in your pocket?"

She grinned. "I wanted to see you light the torch."

They slinked along, the faint echo of their own timid footsteps chasing them. Their breaths billowed out small wispy clouds in the chilly corridor.

After fifty feet, a gigantic oaken door blocked their way. Medieval, all covered with rusted studs and metal braces, with an old iron ring for a doorknob. Derek clutched the cold, slimy ring and pulled. The immense door lumbered open without a sound.

Inside the chamber, eerie contraptions designed for extreme discomfort were lined up against tapestry-covered walls. Derek and Prudence crept along, eyes wide, past a table littered with instruments of torture: a bunch of knives, a spiked metal ball-and-chain attached to a stick, an executioner's ax, two bullwhips and a cat-o-nine-tails.

Derek picked up the cat-o-nine-tails. "I read about this. The British used whips like this during the Napoleonic Wars. To punish sailors."

"Good to know."

They edged past a torture rack, an empty water bucket placed behind a reclining wooden chair, an imposing guillotine and what looked like an eight-foot-tall Russian nesting doll.

"I wonder what this is." Derek pulled on the doll's hinged front. As it flung open, he recoiled from the sharp-looking spikes that studded the interior.

Prudence shuddered. "I know this one. An iron maiden. You step in, somebody closes the front, and the spikes turn you into a human sieve."

"Thanks, not nice."

She stepped around to inspect the back. "Hey, check it out. This thing is branded."

"It's—what?"

"See for yourself."

A small burnt message had been seared into the back of the iron maiden:

PROPERTY OF NORVAL NUSSBAUM

No way. Derek checked out the back of the guillotine, then the backs of the reclining chair, torture rack and table of knives. The same message seared everything. He scrunched up his forehead. Norval Nussbaum's name everywhere. "How does a twelve-year-old get all this stuff?"

"Not only that, where does a twelve-year-old learn to use a branding iron?"

He chewed on his lower lip. "YouTube?"

"Oh. Right. But anyway, his parents must've helped him. To lug all this stuff in here, for a start."

"They must have." Derek waved his arm around their surroundings. "So they let him have this room, filled it with scary stuff. Let him label it all as his property."

Prudence nodded. "Strange..."

Derek peered at the blade suspended at the top of the guillotine. "And now we're planning to help those same parents find their missing skulls? I don't think so."

His brain froze as two gigantic, semi-transparent heads wafted out from the wall at the far end of the room. They swooped up to Prudence and hovered like outsized helium balloons. The man's head gave a kind, pleading look and the woman's eyes filled with moisture. They didn't speak, but floated, waiting.

Derek did a fast calculation. He figured he could run up the stairs in about zero-point-five seconds.

Prudence stood stock-still, gazing up at their faces. A tear slid down her cheek.

"They must have heard us talking about them," Derek whispered out of the side of his mouth.

Prudence didn't answer.

Derek squeaked at the heads, "Can you—can you hear me?"

Mr. Nussbaum opened his mouth. No words spilled out, only a handful of flying moths and scrambling spiders.

Mrs. Nussbaum rolled her eyes and gave her husband a look that could kill. That is, if he weren't already dead.

Prudence stepped forward. "We've been looking for you. Or rather, your skulls. But no luck." Then she added in a smaller voice, "Can't you tell us where to look?"

Both heads shook an emphatic NO.

Derek's skin prickled at the breeze the movement stirred. He cleared his throat. His voice better not break. Not in front of Prudence. "Maybe you could lead us there?"

The heads shook again.

Prudence put her hands on top of her head. "Don't you even know where they are?"

The heads shook vigorously one last time, and slowly faded, looking sadder than ever.

Derek forced his shoulders to drop from ear level. Prudence let out a long sigh. They stared at each other.

Derek ungummed his tongue from the roof of his mouth. "I...I can't believe it."

Prudence's voice quivered. "Nobody would. Gigantic floating heads? Mention this to anybody, and they'll toss us in the looney bin. And eat the key."

"No, I mean I can't believe *they* don't know where their skulls are hidden. Don't you think that's weird?"

Prudence chewed on the inside of her cheek. "Gee, I don't know. Where does Weird stop around here so Normal can kick in?"

"Well, one thing about the Nussbaums. All their body parts seem pretty desperate to locate their missing skulls."

She nodded. "So we have to help them. It's the only way they'll get any peace."

"Them?" He pursed his lips. "You're worried about *them*? What about *us*? Like, they could stop haunting this house, for one thing."

"Yeah, that too."

11

Haunted Halloween

DEREK UNDERSTOOD THAT TO MOST PEOPLE, HALLOWEEN IS A joyous occasion. Well, not joyous like Christmas or Thanksgiving, with people all folksy and cheerful. More like a spooky, creepy kind of joyous. Like, when Halloweeners laugh, they go, "Bwahahahaha!"

But Derek wasn't like most people. He could never understand why anybody would want to celebrate the Scariest Creatures Known to Man and Classic Literature in the first place. Both Living and Dead, by the way.

Yet here he was, putting the finishing touches on preparations for an honest-to-ghoul Halloween party to be attended by a bunch of kids he didn't know. How did he get roped into this horror on the one night he dreaded more than any other? *Like I don't have anything better to do. Homework, for example. Or finding a few missing skulls.*

He kept trying to light the last of thirteen jack-o-lanterns carved by his parents. Mom won first prize for Most Disgusting, hands down, with her imaginative rendition of an off-putting Hunchback of Notre Dame. Eerie silhouettes of pumpkin faces flickered on the walls, giving Derek ice water shivers down his spine.

He was just finishing up when the doorbell scream filled the mansion with its blood-curdling shriek.

Derek trudged through the reception room and opened the front door to a young, beaming pre-World War II flyer. She wore all white, including her aviator's cap, goggles, boots, riding pants, flight jacket and long silk scarf.

"Hi, Derek. Guess who I am."

"Princess Leia?"

"*No*. Look again. I'm Amelia Earhart. Aviator. Author. First woman to fly solo across the Atlantic."

"Oh. Right."

Prudence stepped in and closed the door behind her. "So where's your costume?"

Derek grumbled, "Actually, I was thinking maybe I wouldn't wear one."

"What? Of course you'll wear a costume. It's a Halloween party. It's *your* Halloween party."

"I know, but..."

She crossed her arms. "No buts. Do you even *have* a costume?"

"Yeah, but..."

"Then hurry. The other kids are due any time now."

Derek shook his head all the way up the stairs and into his room. He struggled into the cucumber-colored costume, then stepped to the top of the staircase. Dressed as a giant green frog.

Prudence doubled over laughing, struggling to get out the words, "I expected a prince, not a frog!"

Derek stomped down the stairs—well, as much as webbed feet allowed stomping—and waddled bow-legged across the room. He stood in front of Prudence, scaly arms folded in front of him.

She grinned. "Somehow, it's not even like you're dressed as a giant frog. With your face sticking out of that open mouth, it's more like you've been eaten by one."

"Now you get it," he grumped.

"Hey, I think you're adorable. More adorable than a floppy-eared bunny. Or a kitten that plays the piano. Or—I know—have you seen that video of a puppy riding around on a robot vacuum cleaner? More adorable than that."

"Could we focus here?"

"Okay." She hid her grin with her hand. "So tell me. *Why* are you dressed as a frog?"

"I told Mom I didn't want anything scary. She remembered what I did with those frogs in Biology class, and she made me this outfit. I didn't have the heart to tell her what I really thought."

"Well, I think it's tremendous. You'll be the best frog at the party, guaranteed."

"I'll be the *only* frog at the party. Guaranteed." He let out a small sigh.

Mom danced in from the kitchen, dressed all in black, with a pointed witch's hat and a long, crooked nose. Derek's cheeks burned. What if she'd heard his comments about the costume?

She smiled, though, holding high a platter with a colossal chocolate cake, blazing and smoking with thirteen tiny flames. She greeted them with a joyous "Happy Halloween!"

Derek gawked at her cake. "What's this?"

"It's a surprise. My own special double-decker, super-rich, molten lava, chocolate Halloween cake."

"Wow." He peered at the flames. "And I thought we were all out of candles."

"Oh, we are." She pushed the cake up close to his face. "These are Q-Tips. Make a wish!"

Derek stepped back. "Oh no, um... we should give the honors to Prudence." He shoved his mom in her direction. "What do you say, Prudence? Want to make a wish?"

"No, I'm good."

Mom offered the cake. "Derek's right, it should be you, for all your wonderful work around here."

"Okay, sure. I wish for—"

"Not out loud, dear. Or your wish won't come true."

Prudence closed her eyes and inhaled. Then she opened them again and blew out all the burning Q-Tips with a single mighty whoosh.

"Good job!" Mom beamed.

"Yay," Derek added.

Just then, a shrill screech announced that somebody had pressed the front doorbell.

Mom's smile expanded. "Marvel-oso, your first partygoers have arrived. You kids answer that while I get something from the kitchen."

Derek turned to Prudence. "Please tell me you didn't invite Norval."

Prudence shook her head. "Don't worry. I was kidding about that." She paused. "But he might have seen the bulletin board poster…"

They opened the door to a group of kid-sized witches, vampires, zombies, droids, Klingons, superheroes, ETs, chainsaw killers and one large Donald J. Trump.

And not a single frog.

Prudence and Derek welcomed the kids as they filed in from the front porch to gape at this strange new funeral home. Most of them pulled out their phones to take selfies in front of the display coffins in the reception area.

Several kids went straight to the two open coffins propped up next to the reception desk. Even more inspected the third, closed coffin laid out on a curtained stand, peeking and poking at it.

"Inside, it's a vampire!" one said.

"No, a zombie!" another countered.

"No way," a third kid said. "It's Principal Throttlebottom!"

They all laughed.

Finally, one brave girl grabbed the top lid and lifted.

Derek's gut clenched and threatened to recycle his lunch. His dad lay in the coffin, eyes closed, face white, a wilted lily clutched in his folded hands. Then his eyes popped open. He sat up and yelled, "BWWAAHH!"

Half the kids screamed and the other half charged for the door. Dad laughed his butt off. "Pretty good surprise, huh kids?"

They let out nervous chuckles but gave him dirty looks all the same.

Dressed as a Puritan from the 1600s, complete with shiny black square-buckled shoes, Dad climbed out of the coffin. He centered his wide-brimmed hat on his head. "How do you like it? I'm the witch's husband. From Salem, Mass."

Prudence gave a thumbs-up. "You look super, Mr. Hyde."

"Good one, Dad."

The frilly cuff of his shirt waved as Dad pointed at Derek. "And look at *you*. You're a toad. A giant, green, scaly—"

"Um... I'm a frog, Dad."

"Oh. Of course. A giant, green, scaly frog. Isn't that what I said? Brilliant."

Mom lumbered in, lugging a huge plastic tub with water sloshing over the sides and leaving a wet trail across the floor. "Okay kids, line up. Time to bob for apples. Only, we're out of apples, so we're bobbing for pineapples instead."

Derek's eyebrows went up. "Wait, won't pineapples be too scratchy?"

"Of course, silly. That's why we're using canned."

Derek nodded. "Oh. Right. Much better."

She plopped her burden down with a splash and a grunt and hurried away into the Restful Sleep Room.

Dad turned on some eerie organ music. Then he roamed the room giving kids blindfolds so he could lead them sightless to the Restful Sleep Room and Mom's Homemade Haunted Fun House Tour.

A lot of kids went for it. But not Derek.

More partygoers arrived and soon the whole place pulsed with shouting and laughing over the loud Halloween music.

The front doorbell shrieked again. Derek yelled "I'll get it" and waddled to the door. He opened it to a white-haired imitation of a troll doll wearing blue overalls with no shirt or shoes. The boy's coarse, polar-bear-colored hair had been combed and sprayed straight up.

Norval Nussbaum.

He *could* slam the door, but Mom would freak. Instead, he opened it wider and stepped back.

Norval smirked at his frog costume. "'S'up."

"Hi," Derek managed to croak.

Norval strode in as if he owned the place. He didn't mingle with the crowd, not exactly. It was more like he was a mutton-loving dog wandering into a herd of sheep. Every kid instinctively parted a way for him as if his presence automatically dictated a ten-foot buffer.

Derek flopped along behind him, all the time wondering if this giant troll doll had an agenda. Like, for example, some nefarious plans to ruin his Halloween party.

At the staircase, Norval stopped and slowly turned to look all around the room. Derek ducked behind a coffin. Nobody likes to be stared at. Especially by a frog.

Norval switched into warp speed. He charged up the staircase, taking two steps at a time. At the top, he dog-legged to the right and made for his old bedroom.

Derek jumped into action, bounding after him up to the second floor. Too late. Norval had already closed the bedroom door, then let out a muffled, *"Blue? He painted it blue?"*

Derek ran to the door and burst through, ready to rip into Norval with a short, angry speech about the dangers of trespassing on private property.

No Norval. Where did he—

Derek yanked the closet door open and peered up the winding stairs.

Great. The attic. At night. The hanging string to the naked bulb over his head still swayed from Norval's touch, but the dim light offered no comfort. And speaking of discomfort, the sweat of terror from running in his frog suit made him feel downright swampish.

Bare footsteps crossed the space above. That's okay. Norval would probably toss his cookies when two headless corpses appeared and fumbled their way toward their unsuspecting little boy. Their shoeless, shirtless, overall'd little boy, with his condescending sneer and shock of frozen white hair.

But what if the ghosts catch him?

Derek heaved a deep breath and started up the rickety stairs. As he neared the top, he took a moment before slowly poking his head over the attic floor.

The only sounds were the deep thudding beats of the Halloween music below.

The space was empty.

He crept up into the attic and spun around, expecting to find Norval behind him. Nothing. *Where could he go?*

Derek searched everywhere, shifting boxes, moving magazines, pressing the walls. He avoided the rocking-wolf, though.

There had to be another trap door, another wooden staircase or ladder leading down to a secret room somewhere. If only Prudence were there to help him. All the while, he kept sniffing the air, ready to bolt at the slightest scent of rotten eggs.

Finally, he gave up and dashed back downstairs. Maybe Prudence saw the kid. He should tell her about this, anyway. Not that he needed her advice or anything. But she knew the whole story and kind of understood.

Prudence stood alongside the punch bowl, ladling cran-apple juice into small, plastic pumpkins.

"Did you see him? Norval. He's around here somewhere." Derek scanned the room.

She wiped her hands on her long white scarf. "What? He must have seen the poster."

"Doesn't matter. He's here. I'm the one who let him in. He went upstairs, all the way upstairs, to the attic. I followed him, but then he disappeared. I can't figure out how he did it, but—"

Prudence put up her hand and inhaled through her nose. Derek smelled it, too. Rotten eggs. *Oh no...*

The mirror over the fireplace smoldered with swirling fog, coalescing and merging into the bodies of two headless ghouls, who groped their way out of the wall. Kids screamed, yelled and backed away as fast as they could, all the while staring at the World's. Worst. Party. Poopers. Ever.

By the time the clumsy pair of stumps-for-heads had stumbled halfway across the room, all the kids in the crowd had found their legs and quickly demonstrated how efficiently they could use them to get the heck out of there. They vacated the premises in twelve seconds flat.

Outside, they didn't slow at all, spilling madly down the front lawn and into the night, a colorful, terrified, screaming mob of creatures and superheroes (and one Donald J. Trump) determined to outrace each other.

Dad dashed out of the house to shout last-minute words of wisdom to the departing guests: *"Be sure to tell your parents about the new Hyde Funeral Home!"* He paused, then added, *"And Used Coffin Outlet!"*

Inside, the ghosts were gone, the party over.

Mom rushed from the kitchen, charging from room to room to discover the source of the sudden silence.

"Fuss and feathers. Was it my pumpkin-and-persimmon pie? Because I can take it back—"

"No, Mom. It wasn't anything we did. It's the ghosts. They chose tonight to make a little visit."

"Oh, Sweetie, I'm so sorry. Maybe we should have warned everybody…"

Dad came back into the house and took off his hat. "She's right, I'm such a doofus. I could've made a great big BEWARE OF THE GHOSTS sign. Or maybe I should have given a public service announcement. To prepare everybody for the worst, you know?"

Prudence offered Derek a cran-apple drink. "At least a bunch of kids got to see the new funeral home."

Derek grunted. "Yeah. It didn't *totally* suck."

Mom gave him a big hug, squeezing his frog costume a little too tight. "Think on the bright side, Honey."

"There's a bright side?"

"Sure. Since the party's a complete bust, now you and Prudence can go trick-or-treating. Free candy!"

Frozen Noggins

IF THERE'S ONE THING YOU CAN SAY ABOUT HEDDY S. KIDD Middle School, it's that the young students there are unlike any others in the world. They're kind. Considerate. Sympathetic. Thoughtful. Compassionate. Generous to a fault.

Not.

The day after the scariest Halloween party to be recorded in the annals of the *Littleburp's Hefty Tome of Compelling Anecdotes*, Derek tried to talk his parents into letting him skip school. Only for this one day.

In their usual cheery, optimistic and completely unrealistic way, they gleefully insisted that Derek would have a tremendous post-party day at school. Why, he'd probably be elected Most Unbelievably Popular Kid in School. President of the Snobbiest In-crowd. Kid Most Likely to Host the Most Bodacious Halloween Party Ever.

Then they drove him to school in the hearse.

Even Derek, with his new-found tendency to imagine the worst, wasn't prepared for the level of ribbing, teasing, potent put-downs and outright mocking he was destined to endure that day.

It started with every kid who walked into his Home Room. As soon as they saw Derek, they morphed into shuffling pre-teen zombies groping for their desks and moaning, "Brains! Brains!"

In history class, they poked at his chair and let out eerie "Whooo-whooo" sounds every time Mrs. Caesar turned her back. Which always made the poor teacher peer through the windows expecting a train to come crashing through.

In biology, the students glanced at Derek, giggling as they asked Mrs. Wiggleworm a bunch of dumb questions about the stench factor for cadavers, the timetable for rigor mortis, the lifespan of maggots and all the different ways to dispose of a rotting corpse.

In P.E., all the boys gathered around to laugh as he opened his gym bag to find a small set of coffins and a box of cherry lozenges with a note that read, "Coffin much?" (Later, in the halls, Derek came close to shoving his head through a wall after he heard Coach Noah Thangertu mumbling "Coffin much?" and totally cracking himself up.)

He'd had about enough of this, but that wasn't even the worst part. When Derek walked into the boys' restroom, he found himself in total darkness. He fumbled for the light switch, but several clicks yielded no results. He decided to go in anyway, navigating the sinks from memory.

Someone grabbed his arms from behind and a tall boy held a bright phone screen under his chin, lighting his face with a ghoulish glow. "We're going to g-g-g-get yoooouuuu," he wailed, right before another boy splashed a glass of water at his pants.

They disappeared as quickly as they had come, leaving him to figure out how to find a urinal in the dark. When he emerged, his pants still wet, dozens of kids were waiting outside to point and jeer at him.

Off to one side, the white-haired Norval leaned against a wall with his arms folded. "Have a little accident, did we? I could have sworn you were already house-broken."

Prudence stepped out from behind the crowd to get right into Norval's face. "You're a butt, you know that?"

His cheeks turned red, but he recovered. "Oh yeah? Well, you're a… buttress."

Prudence considered this for a second, then answered, "You're right. I could prop *you* up, for a start."

He had no words. The other kids snickered. He turned and stormed off, pushing several students aside.

Derek was too mortified to thank Prudence. He slipped away down the hall, hoping she wouldn't take his escape from this humiliation too personally.

It went like this for the rest of the day. He never imagined there could be so many cadaver and undertaker jokes.

He tried to tell himself these hilarious kids were only covering their own embarrassment at running away in a panic last night. It didn't help.

At the day's end, he hurried down the street in hopes of heading off his parents. He couldn't handle another arrival of the dreaded hearse in front of the school. Not today.

"Hey, wait for me." Prudence caught up with him after half a block. "Where're you headed?"

He kept walking, head down and thumbs hooked in his backpack straps. "I thought I might join the Foreign Legion. Think there's an age minimum?"

"Height too, probably."

"Nice one."

"Okay, so you had a bad day. You need to get over it."

He stopped. "You know what? I'm sick of this. I'm sick of being a victim. Things have to change. *I* have to change."

"Like how?"

"I don't know, but… something." He stood up taller. "For starters, the ghosts have to go. What do you think? Want to help me find their missing heads?"

A group of kids walking by pointed at Derek and laughed. They continued on down the sidewalk as zombies, shuffling their feet and moaning.

Prudence turned her back on them. "When?"

Derek hiked his backpack higher on his shoulders. "Today. Right now. Unless you have something more important to do. Like maybe learning a tuba concerto, or solving climate change, stuff like that."

Prudence grinned. "Nah, those things can wait."

"What about your parents? Do they expect you soon?"

"My parents? Oh… um… Nope. They're at… um… Home Depot. That's right. They're attending a free class on How to Unstop a Toilet and Not Need a Shower Later."

"You know you'll have to ride in the hearse."

"Are you kidding? I *love* riding in the hearse."

When the black death-wagon drove into sight, they flagged it down and hopped in the back.

At the house, they hurried to Derek's room to strategize. Derek pulled a large piece of paper from his desk and laid it out on the floor. He flopped onto his belly and drew his own crude idea of the mansion's floor plan, crossing out every room they'd already explored with a big X. "We can eliminate the dungeon, the Restful Sleep Room, the chapel, my bedroom—and of course, the attic."

Prudence plopped down on the rug next to him. "Wait. Remember you told me you followed Norval up there and he disappeared?"

"Yeah…"

"So how did he do that?"

Derek sat up. "You're right. How could I forget that? He slipped out of the attic somehow. Not through the attic window, it has bars. Maybe through a secret panel or a hidden trap door. Come on!"

Usually, the prospect of visiting the attic would cause him to spout a creative bunch of lame excuses and masterful delays. Anything to avoid going up there. But not this time. This time he tore into the closet, grabbed the ebony hanger, edged past the sliding panel and charged up the shaky stairs. Prudence came right behind.

His enthusiasm didn't last long. As soon as he mounted the last step and stood in the attic, he sagged. He didn't know what he was hoping for up there, but it certainly wasn't the same old attic, with no change at all.

The military magazines still lay in crooked piles. The gray metal boxes still sported strange black scribblings. The rocking-wolf looked as bizarre and out-of-place as ever.

He stomped his feet in several likely places around the attic, hoping for a hollow sound. No luck.

Prudence moved the magazines and metal boxes around, but the floorboards beneath them seemed no different.

Derek pressed his hands in several places against the faded-paper insulation stapled between slanted attic beams. He didn't expect to find a secret panel that way, but hey—worth a try.

I can do this. Just take a breath and stay calm. With a definite lack of enthusiasm, he edged up to the rocking-wolf. He checked out the head from a respectful distance, then slowly reached out to touch its coarse canine hair. Nothing happened, so he gave it a push. Still nothing. He pushed again, this time from the rear, to watch it rock.

The wolf didn't budge.

He tried again, pushing it several times. The rockers stayed locked to the floor.

"Prudence. Check it out. This thing doesn't rock."

"I know, right? It's not even a *little* awesome."

"No, I mean it really doesn't rock. It doesn't move at all."

"What?"

"I'm not kidding." He dropped to his knees and put his nose down close to the point where the rockers met the attic floor. "It has nails."

"Toenails?"

"No, nails-nails. Like with a hammer. It's nailed to the floor."

"Now we're talking." She stepped around the magazines to see for herself.

He took a deep breath and shoved his whole body against the rigid rump of the bizarre animal. He couldn't dislodge it. He moved to the side. "Help me push this way."

She joined him and together they were able to create a little movement. The entire wolf started to lean over as the attached floorboards lifted up a crack. They put some real muscle into it and the wolf finally tilted over, opening a trapdoor underneath.

"Jackpot." Derek started to gain a little confidence. With a new determination, he peered into the darkness below but could see nothing beyond the start of a wooden ladder.

He looked back at Prudence. "Do you have your phone?"

She whipped it out of her jeans pocket, turned on the flashlight and held it down into the hole.

The ladder seemed to stretch down forever but appeared safe enough. Derek turned around and lowered himself down the first few rungs.

His sweaty hands slipped, but he kept going. "Can you keep the light on me till I get to the bottom?"

"Sure. Then you can tell me who's going to hold the light while *I* follow *you*."

"I don't know. Maybe hold it in your mouth?"

"Of course," she said. "Assign me all the hard parts. I can take it."

Derek ignored her, too focused on making his way down into the room below. Prudence put the non-flashlight end of her phone between her teeth and lowered herself down. "Thsisntxactlyeasy," she mumbled.

At the bottom of the ladder, she took the phone from her mouth, wiped it on her jeans and scanned the light all around.

They stood in a large, walk-in pantry. Old wooden shelves built in front of the four stone walls stood filled with jars, cans and boxes from another era. Derek read a few of the labels out loud. "Petunia Pig's Peach Preserves. Doc's Burn Your Tongue Tomato Sauce. Me and My Big Mouth Spaghetti."

If the pantry contents weren't enough to imply the age of the room, the musty smell sure did. In one corner, a looming, stainless steel refrigeration unit hummed at them. It seemed out of place as if somebody in a time machine had dropped it off as a ceremonial present from the future. He reached over and pulled the door open to a whoosh, a sterile light and a cold breath of icy humidity.

They froze.

Inside were two snow-covered heads, male and female, their eyes and mouths open, as if they'd been caught in a moment of delightful surprise. Their matted hair lay flat and white on top of their skulls.

Derek slammed the door and took a breath. Then he opened it again. He exhaled with a quiet, "Wow."

At first, Prudence didn't say a word, but her cheeks flushed and her eyes watered. Then she coughed and murmured, "We did it. We found… them."

"Yeah. Talk about brain freeze."

As he closed the door, Derek's whole body gave an involuntary shudder. "What now?"

"Yeah. What now?"

He gazed around the pantry. "There must be an exit here somewhere. Norval didn't go back out through the attic, so…"

Prudence frowned. "Wait a minute. There's something I don't get."

"Like what?"

"Like, why are these heads stored in a freezer in the first place?"

"Norval must have put them there," Derek said. "Who else?"

"Okay. Why?"

Derek thought of a few possibilities, then picked one. "To… um… to keep them alive. Sort of. At least, close by."

"But they're not close by. At least not close by to Norval. They're here in your house. Where Norval doesn't live anymore."

"He would if he could. Besides, what else can he do? He can't keep them where he lives now—with foster parents."

Prudence pursed her lips. "He could have had them buried along with their bodies, for one thing."

"True…"

So he crashed your Halloween party so he'd have a chance to visit… them."

A chill shot through him. "Yeah. And then he left here. Somehow."

"Well, if there's a secret door, it can't be that hard to find." She beamed her phone flashlight around the pantry again.

Something caught Derek's eye. "Wait. I see a light switch." He reached into a space between two of the shelves and flipped it on. An antique lamp dangling from the ceiling lit the room. The light was dim but strong enough. Prudence stowed her phone away.

Derek examined the walls. "This switch must be near a door, right? That's usually where they put switches." He slipped his hands in behind a slender set of shelves to the left of the switch and yanked on it. It didn't move.

He tried pushing, then let out a nervous laugh as the entire structure rotated away from him. A narrow piece of the wall opened to a familiar sight.

They were staring into the kitchen.

Fortunately, it was empty.

"Yay. You did it!" Prudence cheered.

"Shh. Not so loud."

"Sorry."

He tiptoed into the kitchen to check out the other side of this mysterious door and found the hidden portal disguised by a tall, narrow broom closet, cluttered with the usual stuff: mops, dustpans, brooms and a small aluminum stepladder. But looking closer, he noticed old tools clamped to metal clasps in the rear: a hammer, a hand drill, two screwdrivers, a hand saw and a crowbar.

He reached in to tug on the crowbar. It was locked in place. "I get it. You grab the crowbar from this side to pull the door open. Sweet."

Prudence stepped through the opening. "I love it. A mansion with a bunch of secret doors and passageways. So cool."

"So *weird*."

Prudence checked the time on her phone. "Anyway, we're doing great. Now that we've located the Nussbaums' heads, all we have to do is dig up their graves. How about late tonight?"

"Late? Tonight?"

"Sure. After your parents go to sleep."

Derek choked. "That's crazy. No way. Go to the cemetery after dark?"

"Sure, what's wrong with that?"

"Well, for one thing, it's dark. Hello."

Prudence nodded. "Okay, we bring a lantern."

"Uh-huh. You do know they bury coffins six feet deep, right? Have you thought about how long it'll take to dig through six feet of dirt?"

"I don't know," she said. "The coffins take up at least a foot of that, so technically you'd only have to dig through five feet."

"Yeah, and we're about five feet tall. So how are we supposed to get out of the hole after we dig it?"

She thought this over. "Good point." She reached into the broom closet. "We should bring this stepladder."

Running out of excuses. What could he say? "Right. A lantern, some shovels and this stepladder. I saw some shovels in the dungeon."

"And I have a camping lantern over at my house."

"Okay."

"And we need to figure out something to carry the heads in."

He shivered. "Carry the heads? Listen, I'm not so sure about this."

"Of course you are," she said. "Everything's working out great. We found the trap door under the rocking wolf, didn't we? And the frozen heads. And the secret door to the kitchen. Could this day *get* any better?"

A Grave Mistake

DEREK WASN'T SCARED, EXACTLY. MORE LIKE TERRIFIED. Horrified. Trapped in a petrifying pit of total trepidation and persistent panic.

Okay, he was scared.

Carrying the Nussbaums' frozen skulls didn't bother him. Nor did sneaking through the cemetery in the moonlight. Or digging up moldy old corpses. It was all those things put together.

What if Derek and Prudence went to all this trouble just to give a couple of otherwise harmless, stumbling ghosts the very heads they needed to see their helpless victims better? What about that?

He retrieved two shovels from the dungeon. It wasn't easy. He opened the dungeon door, rushed down the curving steps, removed the shovels from their shelf and charged back up again. Total time: thirty-seven seconds.

What about skull containers? An ice chest would be too cumbersome. Besides, it wasn't like the skulls were likely to melt before they got buried. No, much better to use a couple of old school backpacks. Then, when everything was over, he could throw them away. Or bury them.

The thought of a decapitated head bouncing against his back as he walked. Made him want to throw up. *Ugh.*

Derek opened his laptop to check the clock. For the millionth time. His mom and dad had gone to bed at ten as usual and were probably already snoring quietly away by now. If only Prudence would hurry up.

Okay, need something to pass the time. Google the Nussbaums.

Nice going, pay dirt with the first hit: an article from the *Littleburp Tattler* described the mansion explosion and fire in the main hall. Police had identified the instigator as the Nussbaums' son, Norval. Apparently, his poor judgment was exceeded only by his creativity—that led him to enhance his chemistry set with everything he needed to build the Town's Most Powerful Homemade Bomb Ever.

As Derek continued his Googling, water splashed against his bedroom window. He ran to the window and pulled the curtains aside. Prudence stood below with a garden hose in one hand, a lantern in the other. She'd changed her outfit to overalls and on her head, she sported a yellow miner's helmet, complete with shining headlamp.

Backpacks and shovels in hand, Derek crept downstairs to let her in.

"Hi, Derek, ready to rob some graves?"

"We're not grave robbers. We're… um… noggin joggers. And cadaver exhumers. And head planters."

"Whatever. Like my hat?" She looked straight at him, blasting the lamplight right into his eyes.

He squinted through his fingers. "Cool. Where'd you get it?"

"In my basement. Where's the ladder?"

"I thought we'd get it after we stuff the heads in these backpacks." He lifted them higher for her inspection. "Come on."

He led the way to the kitchen, reached into the broom closet and pulled on the crowbar. The pantry door swung wide with a tiny squeak.

They headed straight for the freezer, where they stood gaping at the contents for a long minute. Prudence let out a quiet sigh.

Derek wasn't so sure about all this. It was one thing to *imagine* stuffing frozen heads into backpacks, but quite another thing to actually *do* it.

"You do it," Prudence suggested.

"Me? Why me?"

"'Cause you're the one who needs to get over his phobias."

"Oh, right. Throw that in my face."

"Well?"

"Okay." He groped for the male head with his eyes closed but ended up putting his hand in the skull's mouth.

Prudence wrinkled her nose. "Eww. Gross."

Eyes open might be a better plan. He grasped Mr. Nussbaum by the hair, pulled the head out of the freezer and dropped it into the backpack on the floor. It gave off a meaty thunk.

Maybe he could be a little more gentlemanly with Mrs. Nussbaum. He cupped two hands around her frosted skull and gently transferred it to the second backpack. He exhaled. "We can do this."

They each donned a filled backpack. Derek wiggled uncomfortably against the cold lump on his back and then strained to see behind himself. To make sure the head wasn't somehow inching up to bite him on the neck.

He grabbed the aluminum stepladder from the pantry, handed a shovel to Prudence and started out the door.

"Aren't you forgetting something?" she asked.

"What?"

"The pantry door. If you leave it open, your parents will find it."

"That's okay. We already have the skulls, so…"

"Right." She started after him, but then returned and closed up everything. "Sorry, but left-open drawers and doors drive me cray-cray."

"But not severed heads? Weird."

A full moon lit their way across the front lawn. As they slipped past the decrepit *Our Lady of Immaculate Kitchens* sign, a vulture watching them from the top of a chimney spread his great wings and flapped off into the sky.

Derek didn't much like the look of the cemetery at night. Well, or during the day, for that matter. But now a thick cloud drifted over the moon, making everything much spookier. Prudence lifted her lantern higher to give them a better view of the narrow pathway as they wove their way between gloomy grave markers.

The wind ripped what few leaves remained from half-dressed trees. Lightning flashed in the distance. Thunder grumbled at them from miles away, as if to say, "I'll get to you later."

To make matters more unnerving, a skittish owl hooted an ominous "Whoooo?" in their direction while something dangerous-sounding started a plaintive howl.

"Is that a wolf?" Derek whispered.

"No, a werewolf." Prudence flashed a grin. "Kidding. It's only a dog."

"I knew that." He shook all over, but he stood taller and took the lead.

When they arrived at the Nussbaum plots, Prudence threw down her shovel and hung her lantern on one of the gravestone's gargoyles. "What do you think? Do we dig up ladies first?"

"No, age before beauty." He pulled the old green comforter back from the graves and dug his shovel into the sparse, sickly grass struggling on top of Mr. Nussbaum's resting place. He was surprised at how easily the first shovel-full came up.

"While you're doing that, maybe I'll start with the mom. Hey. We could have a race." Prudence attacked the companion grave with gusto.

Derek redoubled his efforts and soon dirt flew in all directions. Their respective dirt piles grew, but before long their energy settled into a more measured rhythm. Well, an increasingly exhausted rhythm.

Ten minutes became an hour. Then two, then three. This could take all night.

Prudence dropped her shovel, gaping at her hands. "We should have brought gloves. I'm getting blisters."

"My blisters have blisters," Derek grumbled. He poked at a fluid-filled spot on his hand and winced.

He was winning at who-can-dig-the-fastest. Good thing, too, because when he struck the top of Mr. Nussbaum's coffin, Prudence was still able to climb out of her shallower hole to lower the stepladder to him.

He brushed the last of the dirt from the coffin, then climbed up the ladder. Wiping his dirt-covered sleeve across his grimy face, he turned to the equally dirty Prudence. "What d'you think? Ready to open it up?"

"How about if you help me dig up Mrs. Nussbaum first?"

He transferred the ladder to Prudence's hole. "So we don't both get trapped down there."

Things went faster working together. It was only after the second coffin lay partially uncovered that Derek thought of a problem. "Hey. How do you open a coffin if you're standing on it?"

Prudence stopped digging. "I hadn't thought of that."

They climbed out. Derek paced back and forth, scowling at the two big holes they'd made. Finally, he had a brainstorm. "Okay, imagine this. I lower you by your heels and you grab the coffin lid. As I drag you back up, you pull the lid open. Brilliant, yes?"

She frowned. "Brilliant, no. What if you drop me? On my head?"

"Like I could be so predictable."

"Exactly. I predict you'll drop me on my head."

"No way. I'll be Wolverine. The Hulk. Spiderman."

"Spiderman?"

"You know, with spidey senses and a really good grip."

"Right…"

"It'll be fine," he said. "Look, you lie on your belly here and inch your way over the edge of the hole. I'll be right behind you, holding onto your ankles."

She shook her head. "How about if *you* lie on your belly, and I lower *you*?"

"That's no good. You couldn't hold me, and I have more upper body strength."

"Yeah, well, I have more *lower* body strength. So if you drop me, believe me, I'm going to use it to kick your butt."

"Okay, it's a deal."

Prudence lay on the dank earth, peering into the grave. With Derek's hands around her ankles, she wiggle-wormed her way into the hole until she dangled close to the coffin hinges. She reached across the coffin and grabbed the edge of the lid.

"Okay, I've got it," she said. "Pull me up now."

Derek hadn't figured on the combined weight of both Prudence and the coffin lid. He grunted and tugged. "Not gonna work… You'll have to let go."

Prudence's hands flew off the coffin. "Okay, yank me out of here."

Easy for *her* to say. He finally managed and together they fell, exhausted, alongside the open grave.

After staring up at the stars for a while, Derek had another idea. "The handles."

"The what?"

"The handles. If we dig a little deeper along the sides, we should get to the handles. That we can stand on."

"You're too smart. I think it'll work."

Prudence jumped up, grabbed her shovel, scampered down the ladder and started digging. Derek joined her and in no time a few glints of bronze bars peeked out of one side.

He dropped his shovel. "I think I can open it. You take the ladder." He helped Prudence out of the hole, handed her the stepladder and stepped down onto the bars. Too creepy. He took a second to slow his raspy breathing. Then he yanked at the lid.

Whoa. A disgusting smell blasted him full in the face. Far worse than the rotten egg smell that always signaled the ghost arrivals. He coughed and gagged, holding onto the lid with one hand and covering his mouth and nose with the other.

He stared over his hand at the headless cadaver. Female, judging by her black dress and the single strand of pearls around her neck. Well, and the fact that she was a solid, meat version of the headless, semi-transparent ghost who haunted the mansion. He half expected her body to sit up and climb out of the coffin. His hands started to shake.

"Now what?" Prudence asked from her safer, much-less-stinky vantage point.

He looked up. "Lower the head down."

She tossed a backpack at him, which he barely caught. He held his breath, reached in, with his head turned to one side, pulled out the head and dropped it at the top of Mrs. Nussbaum's body.

As quickly as he could, he jumped to one side and slammed the coffin shut.

"How did it look?" Prudence asked.

"I didn't get a good look," he admitted. "I'm sure it's fine, though."

"If you think so…" Prudence lowered the stepladder and offered him her hand.

They stood at the edge of the grave and stared down at the closed coffin. Prudence bowed her head and Derek did the same.

"Sleep with the worms, Mrs. Nussbaum," he said.

"Hey, that's not nice."

"Oh. Sorry. Rest in peace, I mean."

He followed the same awkward head replacement process for Mr. Nussbaum, then dumped all the dirt back into the holes. They finally patted down the last shovelful and replaced the old green comforter.

Derek was exhausted but happy as he stepped back to check that everything looked okay. Yes. They did it. This was the best he'd felt since the day he arrived in Littleburp. It might even mean the beginning of a whole new life at the Hyde Funeral Home.

As if on cue, lightning crackled in the sky, noisy with rumbling thunder. The rain that had held off all night arrived in force to turn them from earnest and well-meaning gravediggers into water-drenched sponges. Mud ran in tiny rivulets down their faces, but they still stood there, smiling down at the graves.

That was, until a heavy hand fell on Derek's shoulder.

An Arresting Development

BEING CARTED OFF TO A POLICE STATION ISN'T THE WORST thing that could happen to a twelve-year-old boy.

For example, he could have—um…

No, actually, being carted off to a police station is about the worst.

At least it felt that way to Derek.

It didn't help that Sergeant Bulbous, an eager, round-faced rookie, was pretty rough about it. He dragged the two mud-covered kids through the rain by the scruff of their necks (the only time Derek was ever aware he even *had* a scruff) to his patrol car. Without a word, he shoved them in the back and sped like a racecar driver on fire, careening around corners, directly to jail, Do Not Pass Go.

Then the enthusiastic Man in Blue hauled them dripping wet into the reception area. There they were, a captured pair of lawless grave robbers, staring up at the balding Chief Officer in Charge. The name plate on his desk read "Aloysius Yugoway." Funny name. He leaned over his tall desk to stare down at the newest victims of Littleburp Law Enforcement.

He grunted. "Not again, Flash. What've you brought me this time?

Sergeant Bulbous served up his most official look. "Couldn't be helped, Chief. I've got a couple of live ones here, guilty on three charges: Trespassing in a Cemetery. Desecrating Graves. And Exhuming Bodies without Official Sanction."

The chief officer cast a frustrated look at Flash. "You do know my shift's almost over, right?"

"Wait, make that four. Also Digging Holes in the Rain without a License."

"That's not even a thing."

"Really? Oh." Bulbous stroked his chin. "How about Skull Duggery?"

"Nope."

"Okay, three charges, then."

Officer Yugoway shook his head. "Sounds almost serious. Hardened criminals, by the look of 'em. Little people, are they?"

"Well, littler than me, I guess."

"Not what I meant, but okay." The chief took up his pen and a blank arrest form. "Names?"

Derek sloshed forward. "Derek Hyde. But we weren't trespassing, it's a public cemetery. And we didn't desecrate any graves or exhume any bodies either, they're still there. In fact—"

"Quiet!" Yugoway turned his attention to Prudence. "Your name?"

"Prudence. Prudence Albright." He's telling the truth, though. We didn't—"

"Silence! I need your ages."

Derek answered first. "Twelve."

"Thirteen," Prudence volunteered.

The officer put down his pen to inspect them more closely. "You wouldn't lie to me, would you?"

They shook their heads.

He turned to Sergeant Bulbous. "Did you know this?"

"Didn't think about it, Chief. I saw my duty and I done it."

"Okay, it's a minor detail. You need to get 'em fingerprinted. Also take their blood for DNA testing. Let's find out if it matches any other crimes."

"I can do the fingerprints, but I don't think we can test their DNA. Don't we need their parents' permission to draw blood?"

The large double doors at the front suddenly flew open to reveal the distraught figures of Mr. and Mrs. Hyde. Derek's mom didn't even scan the room, but blurted, "You have to help us, our son is missing!"

"She's right," Dad added. "We—"

"Hi, Mom. Hi, Dad."

"Derek!" they both launched themselves at him, pulling up short as he dripped mud on the gray linoleum.

Dad stepped back again. "Uh… What happened to you?"

Mom stopped in mid-hug. "And Prudence, you poor dear, you're as wet and filthy as Derek here."

"We got arrested in the cemetery," Derek answered. "Then the policeman drove us here in a squad car. With a siren. We were about to be fingerprinted. Oh, and they wanted to test our blood for a DNA match. But then they said we couldn't be tested."

Mom's eyes went wide. "So you're… detestable?"

"Um… no…."

"But you said…"

"I mean," Derek said, "they can't take a blood sample without our parents' permission."

Mom puffed herself up, hands on hips. "Well, they can't have it! No way."

"Wait a minute," Dad interrupted. "This is all going way too fast. Derek, what were you doing in the cemetery at three in the morning? And how did you get so muddy?"

"I can explain," Prudence offered.

Everyone turned to her in breathless anticipation. All except for Derek's mom, who was still breathing pretty hard.

Prudence squeezed muddy water from the bottom of her shirt. "It's the ghosts. We found their heads in the freezer in a pantry hidden behind the broom closet and we thought maybe if we dug up their coffins and returned the heads to their proper resting place, the ghosts would be at peace and they'd leave you guys alone. See?"

Nobody spoke. The seconds stretched forever. Finally, Dad mumbled, "So... you dug the bodies up... but then you reburied them? You left the graves the way you found them?"

Derek nodded. "Well, except for what was left of grass under the old comforter. But that probably wasn't growing back anyway."

Dad reached for his wallet and stepped to the high reception desk. "I'd like to pay for their bail. How much?"

Officer Yugoway looked at his form, then at Derek and Prudence, then at the parents. He rolled the arrest form into a ball and threw it into his wastepaper basket.

"No bail for ruining the grass. It's not an arrestable offense. Get those kids out of here."

Sergeant Bulbous protested. "But Chief—"

"Enough! It's almost dawn, and I'm headed home in two minutes. Don't you have a beat to be pounding?"

"Well, sure, but—"

"Then you'd better start pounding it." The chief turned to Dad and Mom. "I'm assuming these kids won't be digging up any more bodies unless they find some more heads, am I right?"

Everyone answered at once, "Right."

"And *that's* not very likely. Charges dropped. Case dismissed. Go home."

Derek expected the rainy ride back to the funeral home to be either awkwardly silent or filled with persistent questions about their ghoulish grave digging. It was neither. Turns out, Mom and Dad had an adventure of their own they couldn't wait to share.

Mom turned around in the front seat to face them. "You'll never believe what happened, Derek."

"Why, is something wrong?"

"Wrong?" Mom asked. "Well, I've been having a little trouble with flatulence lately, but I've been taking pills, so…"

"No, Dust Bunny," Dad interrupted. "Derek means, what happened that he'd never believe?"

Mom turned pink. "Oh, that. It was a few hours ago. There we were, snoring away…"

"Speak for yourself, Chihuahua. I never snore."

"You don't?" She gave Dad a long look, then continued. "So anyway, there we were, fast asleep, when the ghosts came to visit. They jerked us awake, what with their noisy weeping and wailing. Made a terrible noise."

Dad talked over his shoulder as he drove. "I almost fell out of bed."

"You *did* fall out of bed," Mom said. "Remember?"

"Oh, yeah."

Mom took a breath and continued. "I sat up and yelled, 'Who are you? What do you want?' Oh, and then I think I peed myself, a little."

Dad turned to her. "So I answered, 'I'm your husband and I want to sleep!'"

Mom nodded. "Right. So I explained I wasn't talking to you, and anyway what're you doing on the floor, and you asked who the heck was I talking to then, and I told you I was talking to the ghosts at the foot of our bed."

Dad grunted as he steered around a pothole. "That's when I got up off the floor and into bed, put on my glasses and stared right at them. Well, and also right through them. But the weird thing was, these ghosts had heads. But the wrong ones."

"Exactly," Mom said. "Like, the woman had a man's head. I could tell the body was a woman's, from her designer dress and pearl necklace."

"Right," Dad added, "And the man wore a black suit, but his head wore lipstick and rouge. Pretty scary."

Prudence frowned at Derek as he stared innocently out of the car window. "You got the heads switched?"

"Hey," Derek protested, "It wasn't my fault. You're the one who handed me the backpacks, remember?"

"Oh. Right. But you didn't look at the heads after you dropped them in the coffins?"

"Um… No, not really…"

Prudence folded her arms and shook her head.

Mom ignored the interruption. "Anyway, both the ghosts were weeping and wailing, wailing and weeping."

"And moaning too, don't forget the moaning," Dad said.

"So I decided to try to calm them down."

Dad chuckled. "Your mother kept saying things like, 'There, there,' and 'It'll be okay.'"

"Until they finally stopped their bawling…" Mom said.

"Except for the occasional sniffle…" Dad added.

"And they introduced themselves…"

Derek's eyes went big. "They what?"

Mom gave him a sweet smile. "That's what people in polite society do, dear."

"Oh. Got it."

Mom turned to look forward through the windshield. "So, the ghost with the man's head told us they were Mr. and Mrs. Nussbaum, former owners."

Dad nodded as he slowed through a tight corner. "And that started Mrs. Nussbaum crying all over again. Well, Mrs. Nussbam's head, anyway."

"Right," Mom said. "And they said they were looking for their child, asking over and over, where is their child?"

"And that sounded familiar…"

Mom rotated more in her seat. "So I told them their boy was carried away by the police the day we moved in."

Dad pulled the hearse up in front of the funeral home, shut off the engine and turned around to finish the story. "And that was that. They both shook their heads and then faded away, without another word."

"Which got me to worrying about you, Derek." Mom took a deep breath and continued. "So I said, 'Jack, we have to check on Derek.' And he said, 'I'm way ahead of you.' And I said—"

Dad interrupted. "Well, you get the gist. After we found your bedroom empty, we called the police and then drove over to the police station right away—"

"And there you were," Mom concluded.

They all stepped out of the hearse and rushed through the rain up the lawn to the front porch. Dad grabbed Derek in a friendly chokehold and messed up his wet hair with his fist. "And what about *you*, young man? You and Prudence found a couple of frozen heads and didn't think to tell us about it?"

Derek's mind went into a mad search mode, looking for a reasonable explanation. "Well, we didn't want to worry you…"

Prudence caught up with Derek to walk by his side and add her own explanation. "See, we thought it would save time if we replaced the heads ourselves, instead of involving grownups. No offense…"

Dad grinned. "Hey, I get it. I probably would have done the same thing at your age." He stepped onto the porch, plopped into a white wicker chair and put on his sternest look. "But you kids should trust us more. We could have been a big help. I'm a demon with a shovel, you know."

"And I could've been your lookout," Mom added.

Derek did a double-take. "You mean, you would have helped us dig up the bodies? You wouldn't have notified the authorities?"

Mom gave him a motherly sigh. "Of course not, you silly-billy. What are loving parents for? And why bother those busy policemen?"

"Yeah, but…"

Dad continued, "Besides, don't we always tell you, 'Do unto others'?"

"Of course, but…"

"Well, we practice what we preach. *You* would have helped *us* if the roles were reversed, right?"

Mom gave a short nod. "Exactly. Except maybe not actually touching the skulls themselves…"

"Then it's all settled," Dad said. "You tell us when you find any severed heads, and we'll help you return them to their rightful owners. Simple."

Derek sat on the porch swing and started swaying back and forth. "Well then, I should probably tell you something else…" He glanced at Prudence, who joined him on the swing. "We also found a torture chamber. With a rack and a guillotine. In the dungeon."

Dad and Mom looked at him in silence for a second, then both burst out laughing.

"Good one, son!"

"You're such a joker!" his mom added.

Dad turned to Prudence. "Isn't he hilarious?"

"But it's true…" she protested.

Dad's voice took a more fatherly tone. "Of course it is. And on that funny note, we should probably get you home. You only live a few blocks away, don't you?"

"Oh, that's okay, the sun's coming up and it looks like the rain is stopping. Besides, it's a short walk and… um… I'd hate for my parents to wake up to the sound of a car door slamming."

Mom smiled. "Such a considerate daughter. But you *will* tell your parents all about what happened, with the grave digging and the police and everything?

Prudence didn't look at Mom straight on. "Absolutely. Definitely. I'll tell them right away. Right after breakfast."

15

Exorcise at Home

DEREK SLEPT LIKE THE DEAD. FOR TWO WHOLE HOURS. Of course, not like the Nussbaum ghost kind of dead. More like dead-as-a-doornail.

He managed this triumph of unconsciousness despite the annoying and noisy ghosts who'd decided to hang out at the foot of his bed until morning.

He only woke after the day's first light filtered through his window sashes, along the floor and finally onto his pillow. That's when he learned the painful truth that digging graves all night totally murders your muscles. In places where you didn't even know you had muscles.

Derek stumbled downstairs in his PJs, scratching his backside and mumbling to himself.

In the kitchen, Mom emerged from the secret door behind the broom closet. "Morning, sleepy-head. Look what I found in the hidden pantry. Old soda crackers and aged cheese. There's no expiration date, so I guess they're okay."

"Morning, Mom."

"The cheese isn't at all moldy, but it's hard as a rock, I can tell you." Mom rapped the cheese against the countertop. "I think if I microwave it, it'll soften right up."

"Um… Thanks, Mom, but I'm not really hungry. Maybe I could have some juice?"

"Sure, we have parsley-peanut-pomegranate juice—and plenty of it. But that's not a proper breakfast, mister. I'm the mom, and I say you eat a tasty, nutritious meal. If you don't want cheese and crackers, how about chocolate catfish surprise?

"No thanks…"

"Maybe some Polish toast?"

"What's that?"

"It's like French toast, but I use Polish sausage instead of bread."

"Sure. Sounds great."

After breakfast and a quick minute getting dressed, Derek didn't even mind the ride to school in the family hearse. Because he slept the whole way.

He somehow managed to keep awake through the first classes of the day, but by lunchtime, he felt like a three-toed sloth with heat exhaustion. Or maybe a seriously sleepy slug.

As he nodded off over a bowl of chili, dangerously close to sticking his nose in it, Prudence walked up and kicked his chair. "Hey. You feeling okay? You look worse than dead. You look *un*dead."

"Mmmmmffff," Derek answered.

"Come on, you can't be that tired. I feel great."

"That's 'cause you're a freak of nature."

"Yeah, plus I feel accomplished," she said. "We pulled it off. We restored the heads to their rightful owners."

Derek shrugged. "Sure, if you don't count that we got them reversed. The problem is, we used to have quiet, meandering ghosts who only made small shuffling noises. Now they have heads and we're haunted by wailing, moaning nuisances who can see exactly where they're going. And you know where that is? My bedroom."

Her eyebrows went up. "Oh."

"Not only that, they don't seem the least bit grateful for what we did. They keep moaning about their child."

"So, we made it worse?" she asked.

"A *lot* worse."

"Well hey, we couldn't know."

"Sure…"

"At least they have ears and eyes, so you can talk to them."

Derek rested his head on one hand. "Except I don't want to talk to them. I only want them to go away and leave us alone." His eyes opened wide for the first time today and he snapped his fingers. "Hey, I just got a great, glow-in-the-dark idea. When you have ghosts, who you gonna call? Ghostbusters. Why didn't I think of that sooner? Come on!"

Prudence hurried alongside him to the library where he logged onto one of the computers. He googled "Ghostbusters" with a fresh, satisfied smile—that quickly faded.

"There's nothing in here but *Ghostbusters,* the movie. Useless." He stared at the screen, then brightened. "I know. How about paranormal investigators?"

He typed it in. The overwhelming result listed hundreds of ghost hunters, supernatural societies and paranormal detectives. "Eureka."

Prudence scrunched up her face. "I don't know, Derek. What about the switched heads? Should we be doing something about that? And what about your parents? Will they be okay with this? I mean, would they really be eager to welcome some weirdos with strange antennas and recording devices into their funeral home?"

Derek stopped scanning. "Have you *met* my parents? You know, the ones who said they'd help us if we wanted to dig up any more bodies?"

"You're right. Still…"

"How about if you ride home with me after school? You could help me talk them into it."

"I'd like to," Prudence said, "but I can't. My… um… my parents want to take me to the… um… Littleburp Library. That's right. To scarf up bargains in the Reading Addicts' Used Book Faire. They need to buy seven blue books, nine red ones and thirteen yellow."

Derek's head went back. "Wait, your parents buy books by color?"

"Well, it's not like they'll actually read them."

"Oh." He thought about it. "But that can't take long. Maybe you could come over right after."

"I could, except that after book buying, we always go for Swedish meatballs at Ikea."

"Okay. After that, then?"

"Sure. Right after."

At the end of the school day, Dad and Mom arrived right on time, cheerful as ever. Unfortunately, the hearse's now-familiar *Funeral March* tune also sounded louder than ever.

Derek was busting to explain the paranormal investigator idea he and Prudence had come up with, but he bit his tongue. Better to wait.

Unfortunately, his parents had ideas of their own. "Wait'll you hear what we have planned for tonight," his dad announced. "It's the perfect solution to our little ghost problem."

Derek wasn't sure he wanted to hear this. "A solution?"

Mom bounced on the seat, twisting herself around to face him. "Oh Derek, you'll love it. It's scrumptious-bumptious!"

"Okay. What is it?"

"Exorcism."

"Excuse me?"

Dad raised his voice as if the problem might be Derek's hearing. "Exorcism. You know, where you get a priest or a monk or somebody like that, and they go through a religious ceremony? You exorcise the house and presto—no more ghosts."

"Presto?"

"No more ghosts."

Mom chimed in. "Except, we won't bother any religious people. They've got enough on their plate. We're going DIY on this one."

"DIY?"

"Do It Yourself. We've been watching exorcism how-to videos on YouTube. It'll be a piece of pie."

"You mean cake, Sweetpea."

"Pie, cake, whatever. It'll be dessert."

Derek didn't know what to say, so he didn't speak for the rest of the trip.

At home, his dad led the way into the kitchen and sat at the counter to pull out his phone. He tapped and clicked to get to the right email. "After hours of watching all the best videos on How to Exorcise without Breaking a Sweat, we've developed the perfect approach."

"It's creative, evocative and mega-magnificent," Mom added. "We're even thinking of marketing our own Home Exorcism DIY Kit, complete with accessories."

"Now, Hummingbird, don't give everything away."

Mom pouted a little. "It's all right to tell about the accessories."

"You're right, what am I thinking?" Dad opened a drawer in the kitchen island and brought out a wooden box. "We've got everything a budding exorcist would need. For example," he pulled out a plastic Tupperware bowl with lid, "we've got holy water. Well, to be honest, it's water from the tap. But we blessed it. With a lit sparkler we found left over from last Fourth of July."

"And the plastic crucifix, don't forget that." Mom turned to Derek. "I bought a pretty good one online. I got a great deal. It's fluorescent!"

"Right. And also—voila! Here's a metal tea ball full of flammable incense." Dad lifted it out of the box by its steel chain. You're supposed to light it, then swirl it around to spread the smoke. Kind of like a World War I airplane going down in flames."

"And of course, we have purple investments," Mom added.

"You mean, vestments," Dad corrected her.

"Right, vestments."

Derek rubbed his forehead. "What are vestments, exactly?"

Mom gave a confident smile. "It's like a little vest."

"Well actually," Dad corrected her, "it's more like a purple silk scarf."
He hauled out two long, purple pieces of cloth. "Anyway, you wear the
vestment, sprinkle the water, swirl the smoking tea ball and wave the cross
while you're reading your exorcism script. And we wrote this amazing
script, all by ourselves. Typed it out on my iPhone."

His parents were totally into this. Obviously, there was no way he
could talk them out of it, that's for sure. Derek swallowed and put on a
brave grin. "This is great, Mom, Dad. Awesome, really."

"So what do you think, you're not too tired to exorcise?" Mom gave
Derek her most motherly look.

"I'm in," Derek agreed.

"Okay, follow me." Dad took the wooden box and ushered the way to
the Chapel. With a sweep of his hand, he directed Derek to sit in one of the
chairs set up for funeral attendees. He and Mom went to the podium and
solemnly draped the two purple scarves around their necks.

Then they both took turkey-basting brushes from the box and dipped
them into the small Tupperware bowl. They flicked droplets on the floor
and all around the podium. They even splashed a little in Derek's direction,
for good measure.

Mom lit a match and held it under the tea ball, which turned it into a
surprisingly energetic ball of flame. Meanwhile, Dad pulled out his phone
and nodded at Mom. "The latest version is in the email I just sent you," he
told her. "I'll start."

Mom protested, "Uhn-uhn, not fair. You started first every single time
we rehearsed it. It's my turn."

"But—that's not how we rehearsed it."

"Not fair."

"Of course, my Chick-a-boom. Absolutely, you should start first."

Mom pulled her phone out of her purse, tapped on it several times, then took a big breath and read out loud.

"We demand that every devil, every demon, every ghost, ghoul, apparition, phantom, specter, spook and spirit should skedaddle from this house."

Reading from his own phone, Dad continued, *"We reject every power, authority or curse you may use to mess with, irritate, annoy, hassle, frazzle, bug or otherwise bedevil this house or this family."*

Mom glanced at her phone, then held her arms high. *"We call on all confusion and spite, every sadness, regret or fear to be swept into the Dustbin of Goodbye and Good Riddance."*

"You are released to return to the light, fly into the tunnel, cash in your chips and generally call it a night."

Mom read from her screen in a more solemn tone. *"You are hereby discharged to go about your business and boogie on out of here."*

"You're invited to leave in peace, love and blissful serenity."

Mom smiled. *"With big goofy grins on your adorable faces."*

"In the name of all that's copacetic, A-Okay, too cool for school..." Dad said.

"Cooking with gas, hunky-dory..."

"Hallowed be thy name..." Dad continued.

"Alakazam, abracadabra," Mom chanted.

"Bibbidy bobbity boo and Amen!"

"Sent from my iPhone!"

Dad shook his head. "No, sweetikins, you don't have to read that part."

"Oh, okay. *Amen!*"

Derek stared open-mouthed at his parents. Prudence did the same. Dad raised one eyebrow. "Well? What do you think? Do you feel the lightness, the calm, how clear the atmosphere is in here now?"

Derek nodded, giving Dad and Mom his most encouraging if slightly weak smile. He was pretty sure that wasn't how priests do exorcisms, but what the heck. Maybe this could even work.

Dad let out a happy sigh. "All righty, then! All done. All taken care of. Problem solved." He put his hands in his pockets, then looked straight ahead and declared, "This house is clean."

"That's my hero!" Mom gave him a big hug. Then she turned to Derek. "Who's up for some high tea? Macaroons for everybody!"

They adjourned to the kitchen and sat on stools around the kitchen island as Mom served up elephant-elderberry tea and coconut-crouton macaroons. They were taking their first bites when BA-BAMMM! A loud noise interrupted their feast.

Slowly, they all turned toward the kitchen door as the ghosts of Mr. and Mrs. Nussbaum shuffled into the room, rolling their misplaced heads around and making low moaning-groaning sounds.

Dad dropped his chin to his chest, muffling his sigh. "*So* close."

Cemetery Shortcut

I N THE COURSE OF LIFE, DEREK WAS BOUND TO HAVE GOOD days lifted by giggles and days yanked down by scowls. Bright days blessed with ice cream and dark days cursed with cough medicine. Days with straight As, and days when they cart you off to the principal's office.

Then there are the days that can best be described as *meh*.

Those are the days that don't measure up, can't meet their potential, never make the grade. They're not bad exactly, but nothing to email home about, either.

Today might have turned into one of those days, but Derek wasn't having it. Not this time, not here, not now. Not after all their hard searching and scheming and digging. No way, no how, uhn-uhn, sorry about that.

He slid off his stool, moved past his parents and stomped over to the two moldy intruders.

"Hey!" he yelled.

They continued to moan.

"Hey!"

That stopped them. They looked at Derek in surprise. The head of Mr. Nussbaum's ghost spoke first. "You can hear us?"

Derek pushed his fists against his hips and tried to look fierce. Maybe that would hide his trembling. "Of course, I can hear you, you semi-transparent excuse for a ghoul. You've been bugging us non-stop with all that howling and yowling. What were you thinking?"

Mom leaned toward Dad and whispered, "That's our boy!"

"We thought we were invisible, un-hearable," Mrs. Nussbaum's head answered.

"*Close* to invisible, but definitely not un-hearable," Derek responded. "You guys need to stop feeling so sorry for yourselves. Take a breath."

"Excuse me?" Mr. Nussbaum asked.

"Well, okay, maybe not that. But you need to get a life."

"What?"

"Well, not get a life, I guess you can't do that, either. But stop crying all the time. Cheer up!"

Mr. Nussbaum floated closer, his dress flapping in the breeze he made. Mom started to rise from her stool, but Dad put his hand on her arm.

Mr. Nussbaum harrumphed. "Easy for you to say. What's there to be cheerful about?"

"Well…" They almost had him there. *Think quick.* "At least you have your heads back. That's something."

Mrs. Nussbaum grabbed her noggin with both her male hands. "Do you think so? Is it on all right? I wasn't sure."

"You look fine, my dear," Mr. Nussbaum assured her. "There's just a little mismatch with your outfit. How do I look?"

"Well, your head looks okay, but your hair's a little messy. The pearls help, though."

Mr. Nussbaum looked down at his dress and shook his head. "I remember when I bought you this dress."

Okay, at least Derek had them talking. But he still had some convincing to do. "So anyway, with your bodies dug up and your heads returned, I assumed you'd stop bothering us."

"You're the one who returned our heads?" Mr. Nussbaum asked him. "I don't want to seem ungrateful, but wouldn't it be better to put the right heads on the right bodies?"

"At least we *have* heads," Mrs. Nussbaum admitted. "That's something. Ever since the house exploded, we've been stumbling around, groping for them everywhere. Then yesterday, we could suddenly see. We had heads. With eyes. And mouths."

Derek shot back, "Yeah, really loud ones."

"Sorry…"

"I suppose we should thank you for trying, at least," Mr. Nussbaum acknowledged, smoothing his dress as he talked.

Derek's cheek went warm. "Okay, but now—can't you disappear to wherever it is that ghosts are supposed to go when everything's all cleared up?"

"Ah, but it isn't," Mr. Nussbaum countered.

Mrs. Nussbaum slipped back into moaning, then shot a guilty look at Derek. "Sorry, but it's our child. You can't know what it's like to have your heads blown off and not know that your child is okay."

"Your child is my classmate," Derek said. "From my Biology class."

"Really? And doing okay? If you could bring my darling baby here, even for a few minutes, I think I could rest in peace."

"Me too," Mr. Nussbaum added.

Derek thought about this. "I'm not sure. We're not exactly the best of friends."

"Oh, I'm sure you can do it. You seem like a fine, upstanding young man. Your parents must be proud."

"We *are*," Mom bragged.

"I'll say," Dad agreed.

Derek gave a reluctant nod. "Okay, but then you have to promise not to bother us anymore."

"We promise," Mrs. Nussbaum agreed and held out her hairy male hand.

"Definitely," Mr. Nussbaum doubled down, offering his own dainty digits.

Derek tried to shake but grabbed only air. The two ghosts blushed a light pink, and then quietly faded away.

Derek let out a long breath. "Well, that wasn't too bad."

His dad beamed. "Way to go, superhero. That's my boy!"

Derek had to admit, he felt pretty good about himself right about now. He had actually stood up to one of his biggest fears. Not too shabby. Definitely not *meh*.

When Prudence arrived later that evening, Derek's parents gave her gushing reports about their exorcism and Derek's brave conversation with the ghosts.

Prudence gave a low whistle. "Good job, Derek. Looks like the Frog Rescuer got his mojo back."

Derek smiled in spite of himself. Mom patted him on the head and turned to Prudence. "Won't you join us for dinner? We're having Adventurous Asparagus Delight."

"Um… Thanks, Mrs. Hyde, but I have to get going. But thanks for having me over—and congratulations."

"It's our pleasure, dear, any time. But wait, it's pretty dark out—" Mom turned around. "Derek, you should walk this young lady home. Nudge-nudge, wink-wink."

"Mom!"

"Well, it is the gentlemanly thing to do."

"Oh, that's okay, Mrs. Hyde, I'm fine. It's not far at all."

"No, no. I won't have it said that I raised a rude, thoughtless pig of a son."

Derek blinked. "Excuse me?"

She gave him a loving pat. "You know what I mean, Honey. Now you two get along. And try not to get arrested! Again."

Derek grabbed his jacket from the hall closet. As they headed for the front door, Prudence leaned toward him. "You don't have to walk me home, really."

"It's not a problem. Besides, it'll give us more time to talk about Norval. Like, how do we convince him to come meet his ghost parents?"

"I wondered about that, but it shouldn't be too hard. After all, he already likes talking to their frozen heads..." Prudence stopped on the front porch. "Hey, that's something we never considered. What if he breaks into your house again to visit those heads in the pantry? He could get seriously ticked off when he sees the freezer's empty."

"Ticked off? Try radioactive."

"So we have to talk to him first. Fast. To explain what we did."

"Well, here's your chance." Derek pointed at a white-haired boy in a dark coat, standing across the street. He loitered in the shadow of an old oak tree, staring at the mansion.

"Hey, Norval," Prudence shouted. "Got a minute?"

Norval put his hands in his pockets and sauntered away.

"Hey, come back here, Night Stalker! We need to talk!"

He kept walking.

"It's okay," Derek said. "We'll ambush him tomorrow in the cafeteria, during lunch."

"Yeah... That might be better than trying to talk to him in the dark."

They walked past the old cathedral and Prudence took a turn toward the cemetery gates. Derek grabbed her arm. "Uh... Where are you going?"

"To my house. I always shortcut through the cemetery."

"Uh..."

"Come on, what are you worried about?"

"Not much. But if you think I'm going in there again, you're two clowns short of a circus."

She shook her head. "Jeez, Derek. It's not like I suggested we should dig up some more corpses. It's only an innocent stroll."

"Yeah. In a cemetery. On a moonless night. In the dark."

"Hey, it's just a place to store dead bodies."

"Sure, no problem. They're only rotting, smelly, maggot-infested cadavers. Why should that bother me?"

"Are you still bothered by corpses? Even after our grave digging?"

Derek snorted. "Well, yeah. *Duh.* Aren't you?"

"But it's not like they're planning to claw their way to the surface and take a bite out of your neck or anything."

"I know…"

"So come on." Prudence marched into the cemetery without a backward glance.

Derek gave the sidewalk a longing look. Then he followed her. The evening turned chilly. He slowed as they came close to the Nussbaums' graves, then hurried past.

They walked on in silence. Finally, Prudence turned to him. "You know, you never did answer my question."

"What question?"

"About why you're so paranoid."

"Oh, I don't know…"

"I bet you do," she said. "And ever since you gave me that crazy story about your parents being killed by a killer cop clown, I've been thinking it has something to do with their real death."

"Maybe…"

"So what was it? Were they slaughtered by a demented butcher on the loose? Mistaken for outlaw cowboys and hung by a lynch mob? Thrown into a boiling vat of discarded pig parts?"

"No…" *So many questions. Why can't she leave it alone?*

"Then—what?"

He shrugged. "Okay. It was summertime and my parents were away on a trip. They'd left me with a live-in babysitter, a funny old lady who always wore slippers and talked with a lisp. One day, a priest with a white collar and two policewomen came to visit. The priest sat me in a chair, pulled another chair next to it, sat down and told me both my parents had died."

Prudence screamed and grabbed Derek, pointing up into a nearby tree. "Look!"

A dark figure wearing a black knitted cap dropped out of the tree and ran down the winding path.

As the figure disappeared around the corner of a giant tombstone, Derek caught sight of the tell-tale white hair. Norval. "What in the world— "

Prudence recognized him too. "He gets creepier and creepier every day."

Okay, heart. Reboot.

"So… you were notified that your parents were dead…" Prudence prompted him.

"Oh yeah," Derek continued. "And they took me to Child Protective Services where they kept me in a small dormitory until the funeral. When that day came, they took me to a church. I thought I'd finally see my mom and dad there, lying in coffins. But there weren't any."

"No coffins?"

"Not a one. And I couldn't get a straight story out of anybody. I think they didn't take me seriously because I was only nine years old. They only told me things that they thought I'd understand. And be okay with."

"Like?"

"Like, first they said my parents died in South America. Of a flesh-eating disease that rots your face off."

"And you were supposed to be okay with *that?*" she asked.

"How could I be? I cried and cried. So then they changed their story and told me my parents had gone off on a Halloween-themed cruise. That turned into a ghost ship. In the Bermuda Triangle."

"That sounds random."

"Tell me about it," Derek said. "According to the police, the Coast Guard found the ghost ship without a soul on board. They suspected pirates. Or maybe blood-thirsty ghosts. They could never make up their minds."

"That's crazy."

"Exactly. After that, all I could think about was being haunted by Halloween ghosts. To make matters worse, Child Protective Services sent me from foster home to foster home, each more miserable than the last. That is, until I ended up living with the Hydes. They were great. They were my foster parents for a year, and then they adopted me."

"And that finally made you happy." Prudence said.

"No… I still wasn't happy. That is, not until the other day. When I realized my real parents aren't dead."

"Wait, what?"

"It came to me really fast, like a Nascar video game. See, I was wondering why the ghosts of my parents never searched for me, the way the Nussbaum ghosts did for their son. Because they had to love me way more, right? And that's when it hit me, such an obvious answer. It's because they're still alive."

"Um… I hate to say this, Derek, but…"

"Hey, I know what I know. They're not dead. They're probably imprisoned somewhere, and can't get back to me, is all."

"Okay…" She kicked at a rock.

"So now I have to figure out what actually happened. And how to find them."

They exited the cemetery, then walked one more block. Prudence pointed to a red brick house a little down the street. "Well, this is where I live. Thanks for walking me home. You don't have to walk me all the way to my door.

"No, but I should—"

"NO. I mean, it really isn't necessary. And Derek…"

"Yeah?"

"I hope you're right about your parents. I honestly do. You know your way home, right?"

"Sure. But maybe you could point me in the direction to *not* go through the cemetery."

Mom's Lockdown

EVER SINCE HIS FOOD FIGHT THAT FIRST DAY AT HEDDY S. Kidd Middle School, Derek didn't exactly view Norval as his long-lost bosom buddy. No, Norval was more like a persistent, hacking cough that he really wished would go away, please, and take all that phlegm with him.

He wished.

But, oh well. Maybe, once Norval reunited with his parents, he'd be so grateful he'd never pester Derek and his family again. Hey, maybe he'd even turn into an actual human being.

Yeah, right. In your dreams.

A promise is a promise, though. And since Derek promised the Nussbaum ghosts he'd bring them their child, that was what he'd better do.

At lunchtime, he scanned the cafeteria to find Prudence. If they talked to Norval together, presented a united front, they might actually persuade him there actually are ghosts. Of his parents. Haunting Derek's bedroom.

Prudence waved to him from across the lunchroom. He joined her table.

"I've been thinking," she said. "It's simple. We tell Norval about the ghosts and convince him with evidence. I'm sure he'll make the right decision."

"Evidence? What evidence?"

"Well, there's… I mean… Hmm."

He nodded. "Right. We have no evidence at all that ghosts of his mom and dad are hanging out at the mansion."

"But we have our word."

Derek shrugged. "The word of his enemies, you mean."

"Hey, speak for yourself. Why would he think of *me* as his enemy?"

"Prudence, are you forgetting your classic put-down? I think it was something like, 'I can prop *you* up, for a start.'"

"Oh, yeah…" She pursed her lips. "Then what can we say?"

"We start by telling him we found the skulls, dug up his parents' bodies, added their heads and re-buried everything. I figure he'll be so grateful, he'll be happy to listen to our ghost stories."

She rubbed her forehead. "I don't know…"

"Besides, if you think about it, we all want exactly the same thing. Like, we want him to talk to his parents. This will work, trust me."

"Yeah, but—those heads in the fridge… He obviously wanted them there, for some reason."

Derek nodded. "Yeah…"

"Besides, I think if you dug up *my* parents, I might be a little miffed. In fact, I think I'd be out-of-control, furious, murderous, certifiable… Wait— I see him over there."

Norval strolled into the room as if he'd built it himself. He walked by their table but ignored them.

"Hey, Norval…" Derek waved as Norval glowered and kept walking.

"Want to talk about skulls in freezers?" Prudence yelled across the room. Several kids in the cafeteria stopped talking and eating long enough to locate the source of this strange statement. As soon as they saw Norval standing there, they all returned to what they were doing.

All except Norval. He turned Prudence with a glare and sat down. "What do you know about that? I never told you—"

Prudence shook her head, glanced at Derek, then turned back to Norval. "Of course you never told us. But we found out anyway."

Derek squared his shoulders. "We've seen the skulls. Both of them."

"You found the pantry?"

Derek was glad that Norval hadn't exploded—yet. "Yep. First the pantry. Then the freezer. Then the mom-and-pop-sicles."

"But we've got some good news," Prudence added.

"Yeah? What?"

"We dug up their coffins and returned their heads."

"You WHAT?" Norval stood up, knocking over his chair. "Who told you to do that? Who do you think you are? You can't— You can't—"

He turned on his heel and stormed out of the cafeteria.

Prudence looked at Derek. "Well, that went well."

Derek frowned at the swinging door. "Yeah. I wonder where he's off to."

"Probably wants to sulk for a while. We hope."

"Sulking as opposed to—I don't know—skipping school? So he can go over to my house to burn it down?" *Okay, red alert. Norval did blow up his own parents. What about my parents? He wouldn't—*

Prudence disagreed. "I'm sure he wouldn't do that. He loves that house."

Derek swallowed. "Maybe not. It's true, he drops by to visit often enough. I think he's pretty obsessed with it."

"Let's hope he loves it enough to leave you to enjoy it."

He bristled. "Hey. I never said *I* enjoyed it…"

"Right…"

Derek watched for Norval the rest of the day, constantly looking down halls and gazing through classroom windows, half expecting to see his white hair and stuck-up way of walking at any minute. Half hoping, too, because then at least he'd know Mom and Dad were safe. What was that old line, something about keeping friends close and enemies even closer? No way, that meant he'd have to hug Norval.

At the day's end, Prudence asked Derek for a ride home. He was about to answer when his dad came roaring up in the hearse. But something was wrong. He wasn't playing the *Funeral March*.

Dad leaped from the car, nervous as a lizard on a hot rock. "Come on, Derek, we have to get you home right away. Oh, hi, Prudence."

"Okay if I ride with you?" she asked.

"Sure, but hurry."

They piled into the back. Derek gave his dad a worried look. Has Norval done something? Did he hurt his mom? "What's up, Dad? Why the panic?"

"It's your mother. She's locked herself into the house. And she won't let me in. I need you to talk to her."

"Why would she do that? What's wrong?"

"I wish I knew. She keeps telling me to go away and yelling, 'My husband will be home soon!' I tried telling her over and over, I'm her husband. But she won't hear it. I thought, maybe if she hears your voice too, she'll come around." He sighed. "It's either that, or I go down the chimney."

"Bad idea, Dad. I'm always reading about Santa getting stuck in chimneys."

"Well, I'm a lot skinnier than Santa... so..."

From the outside, the house appeared peaceful. Dad and Derek charged up to the front porch, with Prudence right behind. They banged on the door.

"Go away!" Mom shouted. "I'm calling the police!"

Derek fell to his knees and opened the mail slot. Mom stood in the main hall, wielding her butcher's knife. He put his mouth to the slot. "Mom, it's me."

"Derek? Where are you?"

"I'm down here, can you see my fingers?" Derek shoved the fingers of one hand through the opening.

"What are your fingers doing in my letter opener?"

"Uh… It's not a letter opener, Mom. It's a mail slot. It's me, Derek. Your son."

"Oh yeah? Prove it."

What could he tell her that nobody else would know? Ah yes, the embarrassing story no one else would *want* to know. That should cut it. "Remember the first night we spent here when we all slept in body bags? And you wanted me to wear a pair of my underpants on my head?"

Mom tossed her meat cleaver from hand to hand. "That doesn't prove anything. The bedroom could have been bugged. Nice try, though."

Uh-oh, this wouldn't be as easy as he thought. He glanced at Prudence, wishing she were standing a little further away. He pressed his lips to the mail slot and quietly sang, *"Poopy head, poopy head, don't you be a poopy head..."*

"Derek! It's you!" Mom rushed to unlock and open the door.

"And me," Dad interjected. "And Prudence is here, too."

"Snookums! Come in. I've been so worried."

"You don't have to worry anymore, we're here." Dad put his arm around her waist and ushered her into the kitchen, Derek and Prudence in tow. "Now, tell your handsome husband what's wrong. Why were you so upset?"

Mom plopped down on a kitchen chair. "It was so weird. We got a new delivery today, our second body. A tiny, wrinkled old bald man, a Mr. Shriveldop. Ninety-two years old. Died by choking on a hockey puck."

Derek knitted his brows. "What was he doing eating a hockey puck?"

"Oh, he wasn't eating it, he was playing hockey with his mouth open. You can guess the rest."

"He was playing hockey at the age of ninety-two?" Derek asked.

"Not the point. Try to focus." Mom shot him an exasperated look. "Anyway, I told the delivery guy to stick the body on a slab in the Restful Sleep Room. That was when I noticed the room still had cobwebs in the corners of the ceiling. So I got a ladder and a broom, but I couldn't reach them."

Dad tutted and tisked. "Honey Tree, you could have waited for me. I would have reached those old cobwebs for you."

"Well, I didn't. But I did have an inspiration. I snaked the garden hose in through the dining room window and shot water at them. That kinda worked, but it made a wet mess. So then I got a better idea."

"Don't tell me." Dad held his hand up to silence her. "The leaf blower."

"Oh Jack, you know me so well. That's it. I used the leaf blower and it worked much better, except it also knocked over a few chairs and blew some desk paperwork all over the place. It also made a lot of noise. I guess that's why I didn't hear anybody stealing the body."

"Somebody stole Mr. Shriveldop?" Dad asked.

"Must have, 'cause when I was finished, the body was gone. I mean, there's no way he just got up and walked off, right?"

"Right."

"Which means somebody moved him. So I started looking all around the house. I looked in the Chapel, the Reception Area, the bedrooms, here in the kitchen… Nothing. Then I remembered the pantry behind the broom closet, so I looked in there."

Dad gave her a hopeful look. "And you found him?"

"No. I found a strange, white-haired kid staring into the freezer and crying. He just stood there, letting all the cold air out. So rude. Not a bit eco-friendly."

"So what did you do?"

"I yelped or screeched or something, I guess. He took one look at me and scurried up a ladder into the attic. I chased after him, but I'm not the leapin' lizard I used to be. By the time I made it to the top, he was gone. Probably scampered down the secret stairs to Derek's closet."

Derek put his hand on her shoulder. "Don't worry, Mom. That was only Norval, the ghosts' son. Today at school, we told him how we removed the heads from the freezer to bury them. He probably came here to check."

"I thought of that. He's only a kid, after all. I decided it was a coincidence he was here. Somebody else must have gotten into the house to steal the body."

"But why get so freaked out?" Dad asked.

"Because that wasn't the end. I went through the whole house again, this time looking inside kitchen cupboards, under the beds, in display coffins and body drawers. That's where I finally found Mr. Shriveldop, in a body drawer. I slid it open, and there he was. With clown makeup."

"Clown makeup?" Derek shuddered.

"Yep. While I was searching the house the second time, the thief must have raided the makeup drawer and lathered his face up like a killer circus clown. Not a bad job, actually. A little grotesque, though."

"But at least you found him. I still don't understand…" Dad said.

"Not scary enough yet?" she asked. "How about this? I went to the kitchen to wet some paper towels to clean him up. But when I got back, the drawer was empty. He'd been stolen again."

"So he's…"

"Gone. Missing. AWOL. That's when I lost it. I locked up the whole house, drew all the curtains and grabbed my meat cleaver. Then you started banging on the door, yelling for me to let you in."

Dad gave her a tender hug. "I'm so sorry, Butterfly, I should've knocked more quietly."

"No, it's my fault, Huggy-hubby. I overreacted. After all, it's not like we haven't misplaced a body or two ourselves from time to time…"

"Still, this is too much." Dad started for the front door. "Come on, we can't stay here with a maniac body-snatcher on the loose. I'm driving us all to the police station to report an intruder and a missing cadaver."

Mom went through the door, but held back on the porch, protesting. "But wait. We have to think about our reputation. Funeral homes aren't supposed to lose corpses. We might even risk our mortician licenses if we—" She stopped and stared.

They all stared. The black hearse parked in the street was mostly white. Draped, from top to bottom, with toilet paper.

Stuffed in a Coffin

EREK WAS WELL AWARE THAT GROWN-UPS OFTEN DO SILLY things. Outrageous things. Unbelievable things.

It's true, you can Google it.

Like, you can't imagine how many times a year some trigger-happy tough guy tries to stick a pistol in his back waistband—and ends up shooting himself in the butt.

But Derek simply didn't believe some grownup stole Mr. Shriveldop's tiny, ninety-two-year-old body. And painted his face like a clown. And toilet papered the family hearse.

Nope, those mysterious feats of mayhem and mischief had angry, white-haired orphan written all over them. It was Norval. Had to be.

The important thing now was to find Mr. Shriveldop. Preferably before the authorities learned the body was missing.

"Have you checked the dungeon?" he asked Mom.

"Of course." She clucked her tongue. "There's nothing down there but some old tools."

"But what about the torture chamber?"

Both parents gave him a blank look.

Prudence whispered to him, "They didn't believe us about that, remember?"

"Well, here's where we prove it, then." Derek headed for the dungeon door. "Come on, he must have hidden the body in the torture chamber."

"*Who?*" they all asked.

"Norval, of course. Come on."

The dungeon was *not* his favorite part of the house. He paused at the door, shook himself to relax and turned the knob. As before, a shaft of light from the open door revealed the stone stairway curving into the darkness below. But this time, Prudence pulled out her cell phone and made it slightly less spooky with her flashlight feature.

They all shuffled, huddled together, in small steps down the stairs. Halfway down, Mom stopped them. "What's that?"

"What's what?" Derek answered.

"I thought I heard something out of the corner of my ear." She peered into the darkness below. "Or maybe it was my imagination…"

They continued down the stairway. At the bottom, Derek went straight to the unlit torch at the far end of the dungeon. He reached up and pulled, expecting the stone wall to give way, to swing into the secret passageway they'd found before.

Instead, a nozzle poked out of the wall. As he moved closer to inspect this strange object, it exploded with a blast of wet, white vapor. He stepped back and covered his mouth, but too late.

What the—

He awoke in total darkness. His eyes were open, but he couldn't see a thing. Was this death?

The only sound was his own panicked breathing. *Okay, not dead then.*

He could tell he was lying on his back. But when he raised his hands, they hit something in front of him. Above him. A trap door. A lid. A silk-lined lid.

A coffin.

He pushed, pounded and hit at the silk lid, all the while shouting out a loud string of words beginning with the letter H. "Hey! Hello! Holy cow! Help!"

Then he listened.

His shallow breathing sped up, leaving him dizzy. His heart, meanwhile, tried to escape through his parched throat. And his legs wouldn't stop shaking. But he heard no sound outside.

He had to get out. Anyhow, anyway. He scratched at the silk, but it wouldn't tear. He banged at the walls, but they wouldn't break. He let out the most tremendous, loudest yell he could muster: "YAAAAAHHH!"

Nothing.

Okay, so that didn't work. Good to know. Now he needed to get a grip. He needed to be calm. Stay cool. Chill.

If there was ever a time in his short life when he craved a cell phone, this was it. If only he had a cell phone, he could call somebody. Or text. Definitely turn on the flashlight. Check the time. And most especially, he could google things like, *How to Escape Being Buried Alive in a Silk-lined Coffin.* Or failing that, maybe, *Things to Do When You Have Lots of Time to Kill.*

But he didn't have a cell phone, and he wasn't likely to get one in the next few days, either.

Wait, do coffins have ventilation? He wasn't sure. If not, he wouldn't have days, he'd only have hours. Maybe minutes.

At that thought, his legs took up a life of their own, bending so much that his knees ended up around his ears. With his feet planted deep in the plush silk lid above him, his entire body straightened like a released coil that pushed the lid up, over and open.

He scrambled out of the coffin as if it were full of ants, snakes, spiders and about a million maggots with the munchies.

He glanced frantically around. He wasn't in the dungeon anymore. He was standing in the middle of the torture chamber.

The black lacquer casket at his feet looked familiar. A similar, dark wood casket lay next to it. He was pretty sure these were display units from upstairs. *So Norval dragged them all the way down here?*

At least he wasn't under six feet of dirt. That would have been seriously depressing. A definite low point to his day. Instead, he got to hang out in this perfectly well-lit room, feeling safe and unthreatened. Well, except by the guillotine. And the stretching rack. And the water-boarding chair.

How long had he been unconscious? And where was everybody else?

He went to the big oaken door and pulled on the large rusted ring in the center. Locked. He walked around the room on unsteady legs, searching for clues to a way out. For a torture chamber, it seemed peacefully unchanged from before, except— a piece of cloth stuck out between the two halves of the standing iron maiden.

Prudence had said this contraption turned people into human sieves. What if somebody was in there?

He stepped to the huge device, grabbed the front, closed his eyes and pulled.

No icky sucking sounds from spikes pulling out of flesh. That had to be a good sign. He opened one eye and yelled.

The tiny corpse of an old man stood upright in the iron maiden. With a clown face. But no spike holes in his clothes.

Derek reached in to touch the menacing spikes, then pushed against them. They easily flopped to one side, only made of rubber, as it turned out. *Whew.*

Okay, enough of this. What about his mom and dad? And Prudence? He closed the iron maiden with a quiet, "Sorry, Mr. Shriveldop."

A sudden idea hit him. Two caskets. What if—

He rushed to the mahogany coffin and lifted the lid as far as it would open.

Prudence lay inside, eyes closed, her skin faded to gray.

He grabbed her wrist to feel for a pulse. Nothing. Three fingers against her neck gave no better result. Leaning down, he pressed his ear just below her neck. No heartbeat.

His arms and head started shaking as he wildly paced the room moaning, "No, no, no!"

Prudence wouldn't be in this mess if it weren't for him. Derek went back to the coffin and placed the tips of his fingers under Prudence's nose. He couldn't feel her breath. His hands trembled as he peeled up the lid of one eye. It gave him a blank, empty stare. No life at all.

What to do? *She can't be dead. She can't.* He needed to get help. *Now.*

He flew back to the oaken door and grasped the center ring with both hands. He pulled with all his might. The door didn't budge. He lifted and braced his feet against the wall and yanked harder. No luck.

Maybe if he used something… He ran to the central torture table, still littered with a collection of knives, a ball-and-chain on a stick, a two-headed ax, two bullwhips and a cat-o-nine-tails.

Derek chose the stick-with-ball-and-chain and hurried back to the door. But no matter how hard he swung at the sturdy oak surface, it barely made a dent.

He dashed back for the ax. That worked a little better, but it only chipped away at the wood in tiny slivers. At this rate, it would take forever to chop his way through.

What to do for Prudence? Maybe CPR? Except the only CPR he knew was from TV shows. He could try, though… He raced back to the coffin and placed one hand over the other, just above her chest.

He was about to start pressing when her whole body jerked with a sudden intake of breath. She opened her eyes. Color returned to her cheeks.

Derek jumped back. "You're alive!"

She looked down at her lap. "Yeah, last time I checked. Where am I?"

He let out a high-pitched laugh. "I thought you were a goner. No heartbeat. No breath. Face like a corpse. Eyes like a dead fish."

"Thanks. You don't look so bad yourself." She climbed out of the coffin. "So… how did we end up here?"

"It was that torch I grabbed. Norval must've switched it to booby trap mode. Instead of showing a secret passageway, it poked a nozzle at me that sprayed some kind of sleeping gas."

"Oh yeah," Prudence said. "I saw you go unconscious. Then your parents passed out, then—I don't remember after that."

"My parents." His body started shaking as he thought about what might have happened to them. He had trouble catching his breath.

Prudence glanced at the door. "Maybe they're still in the dungeon. They'd be pretty heavy for him to carry."

Derek wasn't sure. What if Norval was so deranged, he had superhuman strength? "I don't know, he managed to get these two coffins down here okay. Must be stronger than he looks."

Prudence agreed. "And he might still be around, searching for more coffins to lug down the stairs. To stuff your parents in. We should get out of here while we can."

Derek sat down, cross-legged, head in his hands. "I tried. The door to this place is too strong. We'll never get free before he comes back. We're sunk."

She sat next to him and bumped her shoulder up against his. "Hey, that's no way to talk. You should try to be more optimistic."

"Not me. I've decided the key to happiness is low expectations."

"That's completely dumb."

He turned to her. "No, it's not. If you expected Brussels sprouts for breakfast, then you got French toast, wouldn't that make you happy?"

"Sure, Sherlock." She paused for a second. "So, are you happy now?"

"No…"

She bumped him again. "Okay, so how about some French toast?"

He sighed, strained to his feet and headed back to the door. He studied the hinges for a while, then retrieved a big knife from the torture table. He tried to pry the linchpin from the lower hinge. Too rusted.

"It's no use. We're gonna die in here."

Prudence returned to the table to explore for more tools. She pulled at a drawer and let out a quiet, "Huh."

"What?"

"I found a book in here. Some kind of a diary, I think."

"Let me see."

Together they leafed through the first couple of pages. It was filled with hand-drawn sketches of weapons and medieval torture devices. Prudence flipped back to the inside front cover and read:

TO MY NAMESAKE AND GRANDSON, NORVAL NUSSBAUM II

FROM YOUR GRANDPA,

NORVAL I

Derek's eyes opened wide. "Now I get it. This place isn't the torture chamber of a twelve-year-old monster at all. It's the torture chamber of the monster's granddad."

"You think?" As Prudence turned a few more pages, a folded paper dropped out of the diary. She picked it up and unfolded it to reveal a colorful poster showing a bearded magician wearing a black cape and a top hat. These words appeared at the bottom:

SEE THE EIGHTH WONDER OF THE WORLD
NORVAL THE NOTORIOUS

"So that's it." Derek ran his fingers through his hair. "Norval's grandfather is a magician. And all this stuff—" he swept his arm around the room, "is a collection of magician's props kept in here when he was still alive."

"Wait. You think he's dead?"

A cold chill made Derek shiver. "You're right. What if he's still alive? What if he helped his grandson set up the booby trap? And moved the bodies around? And lugged the coffins down the stone staircase?"

Prudence shuddered. "I'd hate to think—" She stopped. "What's that? Did you hear something?"

They both stood stock-still to listen. To the sound of footsteps. As they tapped closer and closer across a flagstone floor.

A Ghostly Reunion

EREK ALWAYS FIGURED THERE WOULD BE TIMES WHEN HE needed to be a take-charge guy. Times when he'd have to take command of his situation. Times that called for a response that went above and beyond all that could be expected of a typical girl or boy.

So he wasted no time in taking brave, heroic action. He threw his arms in the air and yelled, "Quick! Hide!"

Prudence's head swiveled left and right. "Where?"

"Anywhere." He bit his lower lip, thinking fast. "In the coffins!"

She stomped her foot. "I am *not* going back in there."

"There's no time to argue. Hurry up!"

Prudence sighed, climbed back into the coffin and closed the lid on top of herself. Derek started to step into his own coffin, but paused. *Am I being dumb? If Norval put us here, this is the first place he'll look when he gets back. Not the best hiding place...*

He slammed the lid, rushed to the iron maiden and scrunched in to stand next to Mr. Shriveldop. Great. Totally dark. And *stinnnnnnky.*

Just in time. The oak door groaned open and somebody rummaged around the torture table. Then the lid of a coffin squeaked. Whoever it was must be looking in on Prudence.

Derek peeked out from the iron maiden. *Norval.* He slipped out as quietly as he could, tiptoed to the table and snagged a bullwhip. Then he crept up behind Norval. He lifted the bullwhip over Norval's head and in one motion, wrapped it around and around his body, trapping both his arms.

Norval yelped. "Hey!"

"Quick, Prudence, help me!" Derek shouted.

Prudence jumped from her coffin and charged over to the table to snatch up the second bullwhip. As she hurried back, Derek and Norval fell struggling to the floor. She picked up Norval's feet and, despite his kicking, managed to wrap the second bullwhip around his legs.

After a lot of thrashing around and a few choice, animated expressions of his extreme displeasure, Norval finally relaxed.

Derek fell back, exhausted. He propped himself up on one elbow, leaning dangerously close to Norval. "Would you mind telling us what's going on, you fractured freak?" He almost spat out the words. "Why would you want to drug us and stuff us into coffins? What's *wrong* with you?"

Norval glared at the two of them in silence.

Prudence nudged him with her foot. "Hey. We're the keepers now. You're our prisoner. You'd better speak up."

"Or what?" he asked. "You can't keep me hog-tied forever. Sooner or later, you'll have to let me go."

Prudence gave him a wry smile. "That's not a problem. Derek can hold you long enough for me to go upstairs and call the police. I hear they have a three-minute response time."

"Yeah." Derek clambered to his feet. Then, unable to come up with anything more clever, he repeated, "Yeah."

"Besides," Prudence added, "we're not interested in capturing you the way you captured us. In fact, we only wanted to get you connected up with your ghost parents. So everybody can go home."

Of course, *I'm* already home... Derek noted.

Prudence gave him a short scowl. "Right." Then she turned back to Norval. "Don't you even *want* to talk to them? You used to talk to their skulls, after all."

Norval spat at the floor. "Sure, until you stole them from me."

Derek shot him a smug smile. "But they never talked back, right?"

"Yeah, so?"

Prudence put her face closer to Norval's. "So wouldn't you like to have a real, back-and-forth conversation with them? Or at least with their ghosts?"

Norval narrowed his eyes. "Okay... I'd like to talk to their ghosts." His eyes shifted back and forth, as if he were searching for the right words. "But I can't do it like this, all wrapped up, now can I?"

Would Norval really give in this easily? Derek wasn't too sure. "So if we let you go, will you cut out all this drugging and kidnapping stuff?"

"Look, I never planned to hurt you. I only wanted to scare you enough so you'd move out of my house."

"This is *my* house, not *your* house. *Mine.*"

Prudence gave Derek a surprised look, then covered a small smile with her hand.

"Okay, *your* house," Norval agreed. "*Now* can you untie me?"

With slow reluctance, Derek untied the bullwhips, leaving them in a heap on the floor.

In an instant, Norval jumped up and grabbed both whips. He swung them high over his head. With unbelievable speed, he lashed out at both of them in a fluid-handed demonstration of an expertise Derek never expected. In an instant, Norval had wrapped them tighter than a coiled python's lunch.

"Hey!" Derek managed to squeak.

Prudence yelled louder. "You jerk! What—"

Norval leaned against the table with a smirk. "Grandpa taught me how to do that. Pretty slick, huh?"

Derek struggled frantically against his bonds. "You whack-job weirdo, don't you understand we're trying to help you? Don't you even *want* to see your parents?"

"You think I'm falling for that?" Norval retorted. "Like I believe in ghosts. Tell me this, Mr. Beans-for-Brains. If my parents are haunting this place, how come they never talked to me before?"

"Because they didn't have any mouths, genius. If you hadn't stolen their heads and stuck them in a freezer, they probably would have talked to you months ago."

"The same way they talked to Derek's family," Prudence added. "Right after we joined their heads with their bodies in the graveyard."

Norval shook his head like a challenged bull. "Come on, you can't fool me. You want to make me look like an idiot."

"You don't need us for that," Derek shot back.

"Doesn't matter, I'm not buying it. The good news is, I don't have to listen to your lies. All I have to do is walk out that door and leave it locked behind me." Norval started in that direction. "And don't bother to see me out, I can find my own way."

Without looking back, he gave them a sarcastic wave of fond farewell.

Derek seethed. "I'm on fire."

Prudence wiggled in her coil of whips and gave out an exasperated, "What?"

"I'm mad. I'm burning mad. And you know what you should do when you're on fire? Drop and roll."

"Huh?"

"Drop and roll. Hurry. Before he gets away." By example, Derek fell to his knees, then flopped to a lying-down position on the floor. "Come on." He started rolling toward Norval.

Prudence followed his lead. She dropped, lay down and rolled after him.

As they rolled, the whips that encircled them unraveled, leaving a whip-trail behind them both. Norval turned in time to see Derek bump his legs out from under him. As he fell to the floor, Derek jumped up, grabbed his whip and looped it twice around Norval's body.

Prudence did the same with her whip, firmly trapping him where he sat.

"Nice going, Derek," she congratulated him.

At that moment, the large door swept open and Formalda stumbled into the room. She babbled like a frantic monkey, even before she'd looked around. "You wouldn't believe what I've been through. I opened my eyes and saw your dad lying there and I realized he was dead—and I was dead, too. Then something inside me said, 'Go into the light,' so I went down this strange corridor to open this door—and here you guys are." She looked more closely at Derek and Prudence. "Are we *all* dead?"

Before they could answer, Dad came up behind her. "There you are, Juicy Fruit. I woke up and you were gone. Why'd you leave me?"

Mom poked him in the arm with one finger. "You're solid. You're not a ghost." She poked herself in the stomach. "I'm solid, too. Aren't we deceased?"

"Nope. Not so far as I can tell, my angel. In fact, I think we're pretty much alive. I *am* feeling a little groggy, though." Dad noticed the whips wrapped around Norval. "Who do we have here?"

"Dad, Mom, meet Norval Nussbaum. Don't get too close, though. He's kind of a psychopath."

Mom jumped in front of Derek. "You don't scare me. I have a black belt in karate." With one arm over her head and the other outstretched, pointed at Norval, she yelled "HY-YAH!" and made a series of little hops in his direction.

The air escaped from Norval's multi-wrapped chest in a long sigh. He opened his mouth as if to begin a string of insults, but stopped before a single word left his lips. He turned pale and his eyes opened wider than wide. Everyone turned to see what he was looking at.

The Nussbaum ghosts.

"At last," Derek muttered, as the two dusty, bloody, disheveled excuses for a pair of ghosts stumbled in their slow, deliberate way toward them, moaning, "My child! My child!"

Their son wasn't having any of that. *"Don't let them get me!"* he yelled. But they weren't headed for Norval. They ambled up to Prudence and wrapped their arms around her in a ghostly hug.

"Mom, Dad," Prudence gushed. "I love you so much!"

Derek's mouth dropped open. "Did you say *Mom*? And *Dad*?"

Mr. Nussbaum extracted himself from their group hug and said to Derek, "We owe you the world for bringing our little girl back to us."

Mrs. Nussbaum nodded. "Yes, you've been wonderful. We've been so worried, and now here she is, as you promised."

"But—but—"

Prudence blushed a little and spoke past the semi-transparent arms that encircled her. "Sorry, Derek. I wanted to tell you."

"But—you... Tell me what?"

She turned to the two ghosts and whispered, "Could you excuse me for a minute? I need to explain things to Derek."

"Of course, dear," Mrs. Nussbaum answered.

She walked through their arms and put her hand on Derek's shoulder. "My real name isn't Albright. It's Nussbaum. Prudence Nussbaum. Norval is my little brother."

Derek slumped against the wall. "Your little brother?"

"Well, not so little as he used to be, but he *is* a year younger." She turned to Norval. "And you, little brother, you've been a real pain."

"Speak for yourself," Norval grumbled.

"You see," Prudence said, "I'd been sent off to a fancy all-girl school in upstate New York when the explosion killed my parents. The school wanted to keep me there, afraid I'd end up in foster care. But I had a little money, so I escaped and made my way here. When I arrived in Littleburp and found Norval, he hid me in his foster parents' basement."

"But why?" Derek asked. "Why not tell his foster parents you were there and—"

"I didn't dare. Norval already knew they didn't want any more kids. They said he was too much of a handful already."

"But you go to our school."

"Not so much," she admitted. "I try to blend in there, but I don't go to classes. I spend most of my time reading books in the library and practicing in the band room. I thought it'd be fun to take up the tuba."

Derek shook his head. "So you knew all along that Norval's granddad was a magician?"

"Well, yeah. 'Cause he's my granddad, too."

"So let me get this straight. You didn't tell anybody who you were because—"

"Because I knew they'd put me in foster care. Maybe even in a different town. And I couldn't take that chance, not until I knew for sure Norval would be okay. Then I met you and you told me about the decapitated ghosts in your attic. I figured those were my parents. But I had to see for myself."

"And help them," Derek added.

"Yes, and help them." She turned to speak to the ghosts. "Sorry about the mix-up with your heads," she said.

"It's not so bad," her dad-ghost replied. "But if you do get the time, it would be awfully nice to get them swapped back…"

Derek's dad jumped in with his own kind assurances. "It's not a problem, Mr. Nussbaum, no problem at all. We'll help." He turned to Formalda. "Won't we, dear?"

Formalda smiled. "Of course we will. Turnabout is fair play, I always say."

Derek was still confused. He turned to Prudence. "Wait a minute. Why did you pretend not to know anything about the dungeon, or the secret pantry, or the torture chamber?"

Prudence laughed. "We never called it a dungeon. To me, it was only a spooky basement. As for the pantry and the torture chamber, I didn't know about those." She turned to Norval. "Because *you* didn't tell me."

"Of course I didn't. You would've told on me. And then grown-ups would take away the heads."

"Well, you dumb-dumb. Don't you see—"

"I think I can handle this," her ghost-dad interrupted. He stepped past Prudence to shake a finger at Norval. "Young man, you haven't done right, not at all, not at all. Why take our heads? And for that matter, why blow us up in the first place?"

"I didn't mean to, Dad. Honest I didn't. I just wanted to play with my chemistry set. Only it wasn't very cool when I first got it, so I added some more chemicals to beef it up a little. I didn't know I could make explosions. And afterward, I took your heads so I could put them with your bodies. But then they buried your bodies. And I missed you—a *lot*—so..."

"I understand, Norval," his ghost-mom said. "But you do know it was wrong, don't you?"

He bowed his head. "I do now... I'm sorry..."

"Me too," Prudence added, turning back to Derek. "I'm sorry I didn't tell you who I was."

"Yeah." Derek gave her his most hurt look. "You should've trusted me."

"You're right," she said. "But I'll make it up to you. Somehow."

"Well, isn't this nice," Mom gurgled. "Now you have your family back, all together and full of love. And you'll live happily ever after."

"Well, almost," Derek objected.

"What do you mean, Son?" his dad asked.

"Prudence still doesn't have a home. After all, she can't keep living in secret in Norval's basement."

Mom brightened and put her finger in the air. "We have plenty of room. In fact, Prudence could be your sister."

Derek tried not to smile. "Really?"

"You mean it?" Prudence looked at her ghostly parents. "Would that be okay with you?"

"Of course, Sweetheart," Mr. Nussbaum assured her.

"You know it is," Mrs. Nussbaum added.

"You're sure?" Prudence asked.

"We're sure," they both answered.

Mom tilted her head to one side. "Awww."

Without another word, the ghosts faded away. After they were gone, Derek could have sworn he heard a faint "Thank you…"

"Well," Mom said, smoothing her skirt. "All's well that ends well—and all that jazz."

Dad looked around the room. "So. Not to change the subject or anything, but—has anybody seen Mr. Shriveldop?"

Body Parts

BY THE NEXT SATURDAY, EVERYTHING HAD RETURNED TO normal. Well, not normal, exactly. More like abnormal.

Derek's parents had fixed up a room for Prudence and made all the necessary arrangements to sign up as her foster parents. But then Norval mysteriously disappeared. Rumors around the school had him variously jumping a freight train, stealing a little kid's bicycle, hitchhiking on the freeway, and hiding in the wheel well of a FedEx plane at Littleburp Airport.

Derek wasn't so sure. He figured Norval could still be around, still lurking near the funeral home. So he could be near Prudence and their ghostly parents. Or maybe not.

"You know," his mom mused, "if he does show up, we could always offer to be *his* foster parents, too."

"Wait, what?" Derek sputtered, dribbling a mouthful of yak milk onto the kitchen counter.

"That way, you'd have a brother. And he could talk to his ghost parents whenever he wanted to. Wouldn't that be nice?"

"Um… no. I don't think he'd be happy here, Mom."

"Why not? Don't you think we'd be better for him than being on the run somewhere?"

Derek stood up from his stool to walk over to his mother and wrapped his arms around her. "You know what, Mom?" he said. "I totally love you."

Her eyes teared up. "You do?"

He nodded. "I really do. You're the most... unique mom in the whole world. And I love you for being you. And Dad, too."

She sniffled, then turned away. "I must do something about these kitchen tiles," she said. "Have you noticed how they get dirty about once a week?"

Derek turned and waved behind his head, heading out the door. "I have to help Dad. I finally convinced him to remove the second half of that sign out front."

"Have fun, dear."

As he stepped outside, his dad finished opening the second of two tall aluminum ladders under the dual sign above the front porch that read:

HYDE FUNERAL HOME &
USED COFFIN OUTLET

"I have to say," Dad admitted, "you were right. The last half of this sign wasn't helping business at all. Especially since we never actually got any used coffins to sell."

"Glad to hear it, Dad."

Prudence rode up the front path on her bicycle. "Hi, Derek. Hi, Dad."

"Hi, Prudence," Dad said. "Want to see something cool?"

"Sure. What're you guys doing?"

"Taking down the lower part of the sign," Derek explained.

"If you kids can hang out on the porch swing for a minute," Dad added, "I have to get something from the hearse."

Prudence dropped her bike and joined Derek on the swing. "You know Derek, you surprised me."

"How? When?"

"Remember when we had Norval all wrapped up? And you yelled at him? You yelled that this is *your* house, not *his*—even after a long time of hating this place."

"Yeah…"

"Then you were really nice to my parents, even after they haunted you. Even after all that moaning and groaning."

"Yeah…"

"So the next thing I know, you'll be saying you like your school."

Derek rocked the swing. "Well, I do, sort of."

"What?"

"Well, maybe 'like' is a little strong. But after a while, it kind of grew on me, you know? Like a fungus."

As they sat swinging, Prudence brought up a ticklish subject. "Would you help me find Norval? He is my brother, after all."

Derek thought about this for a second, then admitted, "Of course I will."

"Cool. And I'll help you."

"With—"

"Well, I've been thinking about your original parents. I mean, it's obvious that you care for the Hydes, but—are you still imagining that your birth parents are alive? I mean, actually alive?"

"Well, yeah." He thought for a second. "Don't get me wrong. I'm happy to be here, and really grateful for my new mom and dad. After all, I've been with them for a while now. And even though they're a little off-beat—well, a *lot* off-beat—they'll always be great parents, no matter what else happens. But still…"

"Still?"

"Still, I can't help thinking my real parents are out there somewhere. And somehow, I plan to find them. I only have to figure out how."

"Well, I wanted you to know, I believe you."

"You do?"

"Sure. If you feel so strongly about it, I should trust you. And if you need my help to search for them, you can count me in."

"Thanks. You know—"

Dad reappeared, carrying a large package. "Well, here it is, kids."

"Here's what, Dad?"

"Well, I decided to do a little moonlighting while we're getting our funeral business up and running. I'm good at fixing cars, so I thought I could use my spare time to start a little car repair business on the side."

"That's great, Dad," Derek said. "Maybe you could even teach us about cars."

"Be glad to, my boy."

"But what's in the package?" Prudence asked.

Dad beamed. "Right. It's a replacement for the second half of that sign up there, to promote my *new* sideline. Derek, you want to help me get the old sign down first?"

"Sure…"

It only took a couple of minutes, a little grunting and a lot of huffing and heaving, but they managed to remove it. Dad insisted they erect the new sign with the brown paper packaging still on it so he could do an official "reveal."

Erecting the new sign took a little longer, but they finally got it into place.

"Now, you kids stand in the yard and close your eyes. So you can get the full effect." They did as he suggested while he went back up the ladder to pull off the paper.

"Okay, open your eyes."

With the paper off, the full sign now read,

HYDE FUNERAL HOME &
BODY PARTS SHOP

Prudence broke into a huge grin.

Derek put his head in his hands and let out a small, almost imperceptible whimper.

– THE END –

Acknowledgments

I have many people to thank, but first and foremost my heartfelt and undying gratitude goes to my incredible wife, Merlyn, whose constant love and support continue to amaze me.

A number of beta readers and critique partners gave me invaluable feedback and suggestions for improvement, including my brilliant sisters Dustie Lynch and Nancy Harris; awesome writers John Boykin, Léonie Kelsall, Rebecca Petruck, Kortney Price, Jason Robins, Bronwyn Deaver, Miranda Shevertalov, Pat Correll and Sam Subity; and my unbelievable mentors from the Write-Mentor program, Emma Finlayson-Palmer and Carolyn Ward.

I would also like to acknowledge my agent for the Derek Hyde series, Patty Carothers of Metamorphosis Literary, for her untiring dedication and enthusiastic support in promoting my work to publishers.

Thank you for reading!

If you enjoyed Derek Hyde Knows Spooky When He Sees It, please leave a review to help other readers discover it.

About the Author

E. Michael Lunsford is the author of an award-winning play, *Scary, Scary Night*, and a book of wacky kid's poems, *Sometimes I Get My Shoes on Backwards*, winner of the Readers' Favorite International Book Award. His debut novel is the first of the funny Derek Hyde series of spooky middle grade books published by INtense Publications. Michael is also a musician, composer, inventor, entrepreneur and chief cook & bottle washer who works with his wife and love of his life in San Carlos, California.

Continue reading for Book 2 in
the Derek Hyde series.

Derek Hyde's Spooky Scavenger Hunt

By

E. Michael Lunsford

Chapter 1
Littleburp Cemetery

DEREK COULDN'T BELIEVE HE AND PRUDENCE WERE— once again—sneaking into the graveyard to dig up bodies. At midnight.

The last time they did that, a policeman nabbed them. They'd come *this close* to being thrown in the pokey.

But it wasn't Derek's idea. He wasn't at all ready to go back. Not yet, anyway. It's just that Prudence insisted. She kept complaining they'd waited long enough. They couldn't put it off anymore.

So, there they were, following the beams of their flashlights past *Our Lady of Immaculate Kitchens*—the old abandoned church next to the funeral home where they lived—and trudging toward the big metal gate that dangled on rusty hinges in front of the Littleburp Cemetery.

When the headlights of a police car swept across the graveyard wall, Prudence ducked behind a bush. Derek managed to hide behind a mailbox before the car finished its slow turn onto Slimytoes Lane. They both watched as it crept down the street and disappeared into the darkness.

Even in the chilly evening air, sweat ran down Derek's back. He couldn't stop shaking. He wasn't sure if it was more from the police car or the spookiness of it all. Probably both.

So okay, he panicked. It wasn't so much his dry mouth or his trip-hammering heart. He just couldn't catch his breath. He was breathing, all right, exhaling little clouds of wet steam. Or maybe wheezing was a better word. But it didn't help. He was suffocating.

Prudence stepped out from behind the bush into the yellow pool of light of an old streetlamp. She looked back to see Derek all bent over, his hands on his kneecaps.

"Come on," she whispered. "Why are you dragging your feet? We don't have all night, you know."

"Can't... breathe..."

She dropped her shovel and rushed back to his side. "Are you okay? Anything I can do?" She squatted next to him and put her hand on his back.

"Oxygen... mask..." he huffed. "Scuba... tank..." he puffed. "Iron... lung..."

Prudence stood up. "Now you're just being silly. Where would I get those things at midnight? What you need is a paper bag to breathe into."

"Yes... paper bag..."

She swung the backpack from her shoulders and rummaged through its contents. "This should do the trick." She dug out a small, pink, polka-dotted shopping bag and handed it over.

Derek smashed the bag opening to his face and panted into it. The bag inflated and deflated like a blowfish. After a while, his breathing slowed.

"All better?" Prudence was frowning, but he couldn't tell if her look came from worry or impatience.

"I think I'm okay now..."

How did she always manage to be so much more fearless than he was? It was embarrassing. Especially since she was only thirteen—just a year older than him.

He sighed, picked up his shovel, adjusted his backpack and followed her into the scariest boneyard in Littleburp.

At least they had a full moon. A scowling, pale white moon with occasional bats flying across its face. That moon seemed awfully good at casting creepy shadows of leafless trees onto their path.

Derek scurried to catch up with Prudence, trying hard to ignore his shivering. And the hair that stood up on the back of his neck.

She finally broke from the path to stride onto the grass, leaving a trail of dark green footprints in the early winter frost.

"Here they are." She dropped down next to a pair of graves. "I hope the ground isn't too hard."

Derek leaned against one of the tombstones, but quickly recoiled at the surprising cold. "It shouldn't be too bad," he suggested. "It's only been six weeks since the last time we dug them up. I bet the dirt's still loose."

"Good point." She smiled. "How about if you take my dad's grave and I'll dig up my mom. I'll race you."

That was Prudence all over. She made a game out of it, to take his mind off the gruesome effort ahead of them. And it worked. He dove right in (so to speak) and before long had shoveled out a nice big pile of dirt.

Prudence's pile was almost as big, but he was ahead so far. He redoubled his efforts. There was no way he'd lose this contest. She was sure to be impressed. He worked so hard that he didn't hear footsteps coming up from behind.

"Oy! What're you two young cockatoos doin' down there?"

They both jerked their heads up to see a scrawny man in ragged pants, rubber boots and a navy peacoat, holding a lantern high above his head. He had sunken cheeks and tufts of white hair peeked out from under his smudged top hat.

Derek shaded his eyes from the glare of the lantern. "Who, us?" he stammered, mostly for something to say.

"Too right, I mean you. Who said you could dig up the flippin' grass like that?"

"Well…" Derek climbed out of his hole. "You see…"

"It's for the mushrooms," Prudence interrupted. She climbed up to join Derek and put the backs of her hands on her hips. "Didn't you get the text?"

The man swung around to face her. "Text? What blinkin' text?"

"From the mayor," she said, not missing a beat. "It was sent out to all cemetery personnel, two days ago."

"Looky here, I'm the grounds keeper—"

"You are?" Prudence asked.

"'Course I am. Durwood Didgeridoo, that's me, from Down Under. Also known as Re-do. But you can call me Digger. And I didn't get any ruddy text."

"Oh, well, that explains everything." Prudence dropped her hands to her side. "Must have been a problem with um… the internet. Well, not to worry, I can explain it all. You see…" She paused as Derek snuck up behind Digger, shovel high in the air, ready to bonk his lights out. "Wait!" she yelled.

"Wait?" Digger gave her a curious look. "For what?"

"Uh… For me to… um… remember the exact words of the text," she stammered.

Digger put his lantern down, almost on Derek's foot. Derek stepped back as quietly as he could.

"Oh, right. I remember," she said. "It was an announcement about the… um… nocturnal mushrooms. They have to be dug up exactly at midnight tonight, or… or… they won't be any good."

"Nocturnal *what* rooms?"

"Mushrooms," Derek echoed. He sauntered out from behind Digger as casually as he could. "You know, those little, brown, musty things that grow underground?"

"It's like this," Prudence continued. "The mayor held a lottery to pick who would get to dig up the mushrooms. And Derek and I won. It was all in the text."

"Exactly," Derek said. "We couldn't believe our amazing luck. Imagine, two kids being picked out of all those applicants."

The man's forehead scrunched up. "But I never—"

Prudence gave him a sly look. "Of course, if you don't believe us, you could always phone the mayor…"

"Right," Derek added. "I'm sure he won't mind being yanked out of a good night's sleep to take your call. Prudence is right, you should call him. Can't be too careful, these days."

"Well, now, hold on a sec." Digger paced back and forth, his hands behind his back, talking to himself. "If I ring his honor up and they're lyin', I'll be a hero. But if they're tellin' the truth, I'll be a bloomin' nincompoop." He stopped pacing and repeated, "Hero. Nincompoop. Hero. Nincompoop."

"I don't think I'd go for Hero," Prudence suggested.

"Not if it makes you a nincompoop," Derek added.

Digger gave a firm nod. "Got it. Congratulations, you two. I reckon you'll find lots and lots of mushrooms. Be sure to put the grass back when you tidy up. G'night!"

He picked up his lantern, turned on his heel and strode off into the dark. As he walked, he glanced several times at the sky, then muttered to himself,

Bats! Bats! Flyin' rats!

Bats in yer belfry,

Bats in yer hats!

Flittin' and flutterin'

Winged acrobats!

Thousands and thousands

And thousands of bats!

This didn't exactly lighten Derek's mood.

When the ground keeper's lantern finally blinked out of sight, Prudence broke into a big grin. "What a crazy guy."

"Crazy," Derek repeated.

"And what about *you*, sneaking up behind him? I was worried there for a minute you might bash his brains in."

He gave her a weak smile. "Sorry. I should have guessed you'd come up with a good story." He picked up his shovel. "We'd better hurry up and finish our digging before that guy decides to google Nocturnal Mushrooms."

Unfortunately, all the hurry in the world couldn't reduce the amount of work ahead of them. It took hours before they finally got the coffins uncovered.

Prudence pulled two surgical masks out of her hip pocket and tossed one to Derek. "For the stink," she said.

He put his mask on and with trembling, dirty hands, lifted the coffin lid. The overwhelming stench came at him like a dense fog. He almost gagged, but somehow managed to hold it together.

He stared at the cadaver. That was definitely Prudence's father, Mr. Nussbaum. At least, that was him from the neck down. From the pearl necklace up, it was *Mrs.* Nussbaum. Derek blushed to remember how he got the heads switched last time.

He rubbed his hands on his pants, then tenderly lifted Mrs. Nussbaum's head out of the coffin and passed it up to Prudence—who handed down her father's. As creepy as this all felt, Derek was washed by a huge relief to see the corpse whole again, with Mr. Nussbaum's head in its rightful place at the top of his body. He slammed the coffin shut and scampered out of that hole as fast as he could.

Prudence had done the same with Mrs. Nussbaum's head in her coffin. It was much faster filling the graves back up again. Just as the morning sun peeked over a nearby hill, they finished patting the last of the grass sod on top.

It was a good thing, too. Only a minute later, Prudence caught a glimpse of Digger headed back their way.

"Oh-oh," she said. "Seems like Digger might have looked up Nocturnal Mushrooms after all."

"I'm right behind you." Derek slung his backpack onto his shoulders, grabbed his flashlight and shovel, and ran.

Unfortunately, so did Digger. And he was gaining on them. Prudence took a hard left at a mossy crypt and Derek followed as best he could. He caught glimpses of her weaving between tall gravestones and crosses, then lost sight of her entirely.

Meanwhile, Digger was closer than ever. "Oy! I need a word! Hold up there, you two!"

Derek slid under a large wreath of dying flowers propped on a wooden easel and scrambled behind an old tombstone.

Digger went charging past, came to a split in the path, stopped, looked both ways, and scratched his head. Then he rushed to the left, once again yelling, "Oy! Oy!"

"Good job," came a whisper in his ear. Derek swiveled around to face Prudence. He couldn't imagine how she managed to double back like that.

"Let's get out of here." She sprinted down the way they had come.

Derek started to join her, but one foot gave out and he fell on his face.

"Wait," he shouted through a mouthful of grass. "My ankle."

Prudence pulled up short and rushed to his side. "What did you do? Is it twisted?"

"I think so."

"Here, I'll help. Put your arm around my shoulder."

He leaned on Prudence, who started to pull him up. Then she stopped and dropped him to the ground again.

"Did you see this?" she pointed a shaky finger at the tombstone behind him.

"See what?" Derek craned his neck to see what she was talking about.

"This." She rubbed at the dirt on the grave marker.

Derek squinted to read the words:

Durwood
Didgeridoo

1946 – 2009

I told you I was sick.

I dug those holes
From stem to stern
Dumped the bodies in—

Below the inscription he could barely make out a short poem:

> *I dug those holes*
>
> *From stem to stern*
>
> *Dumped the bodies in—*
>
> *Now it's my turn*

Derek's eyes went big. "You don't suppose—"

Prudence nodded. "Exactly. This is Digger's grave. The grounds keeper."

"Which means—"

"He's dead. And we're being chased by his ghost."

Derek gulped. "And when he said he was from Down Under…"

"We thought he meant Australia."

"Oy!" came a voice from the darkness.

"Yow!" they both shouted. Prudence helped Derek to his feet and they hurriedly hobbled their way toward the graveyard wall.

Derek tried to fight down his rising panic. "Don't slow down!" he gasped to Prudence. "If we can get free of the cemetery, the ghost can't follow. I hope."

They hopped, tripped and stumbled down the path and through the cemetery gate—where they collapsed on the sidewalk.

"I think we're safe now," Derek panted. "I just need to rest a second." He scooted to the curb to rub his ankle and Prudence joined him. It wasn't until Derek leaned back that he noticed a couple of black, polished shoes that clearly belonged to somebody standing right behind him.

CPSIA information can be obtained
at www.ICGtesting.com
Printed in the USA
FSHW020729250120
66401FS